You Made
Me Smile

Mélissa Délalie Houinsou

ISBN 978-1-9701-0970-2

Published August 2021

ANEWPRESS

ABOUT THE AUTHOR

Two-time winner of the Universal Postal Union International Letter-Writing competition, Mélissa Délalie Houinsou is a young writer born in 2001 in Cotonou, Benin. A lover of writing, she is also a health sciences student at the University of Ottawa. She won a 2019 Watty Award in the New Adult category.

DEDICATION

To those who give love,
to those who need love,
to my lovely family.

ACKNOWLEDGEMENTS

Writing this book was a way to heal myself through a difficult period and I hope it heals even the littlest broken part of your lives. I would like to thank my parents who give me unconditional love and support through every step I take. A special thanks to my friend Hayat who helped me keep my love of writing alive over the years, read all my drafts and gave me cheers when needed. To Annabelle, Lucrece and Vivien who particularly believed in me and encouraged me in the journey of *You made me smile*, I want you to know how much I value your confidence in my capacities. To all those who once read me or supported me in any other way, I give my deepest thanks.

Prologue

For some, I am the depressed girl. Meanwhile for others, I am the lost girl. I am Fifame Lawson, some people may refer to me as a sad or instable person. Since that day in elementary school, the day everything changed, something broke inside me. I have been through depression for years. How am I doing now? Very well, at least this is what I tell everyone. The secret between the night, my pillow and my bed are another deal. They are the only "people" aware of the reality. Throughout those painful years, I could no longer eat — I was thinner than a rake, I smiled barely, I was always sick. To sum up, I was the shadow of myself… I still am. There are so many incurable diseases, but depression is the strongest one. No one can help me, and I can't promise anything to anyone. I just have to live with it, with my best friend, depression. Today I am better, I am used to her… And I don't notice her any more. Depression has become mine. In fact, I have become hers.

CHAPTER ONE

A fter dinner, I help my mother to clean up: plates and bowls straight in the dishwasher after neatly conserving the eatable rest of foods in the fridge and glasses washed directly to keep their brightness. Father is sitting on a chair, sipping his coffee and reading for the hundredth time the same magazine about architecture. He narrows his eyes as if to catch any detail. I kiss mother on the cheek and then hug father who barely looks at me. I sometimes think he loves more architecture than me. They finally smile to me and wish me goodnight. I reach my room, put on my big pajamas —a long pant and a shirt with Naruto' characters drawn all over them — and throw myself onto bed. My smile falls and tears take over my face as I feel that emptiness filling my heart.

Same story, same routine. Smile the day and cry the night, no one knows it. I switch the light off with an impatient move before lying back down roughly. As I am staring at the ceiling through the twilight, I startle when my phone beeps. I grab it without excitement, sit and scroll the screen, in search of any meaningful news. I don't like social networks; they make me sad. I hate to see those perfect lives through my screen. I have a wonderful family, great friends (big joke) but I still feel bad, always bad. The only picture on my Instagram profile appears. My parents took it for my last birthday. I was sitting on the couch and smiling, at least trying.

Looking so happy but so sad is sad.

I frown while reading the text from someone called Yourlight.

What are you talking about?

I couldn't help but reply.

Your pic, why do you look so sad on it?

I wonder too. But at the same time, the answer is as clear as a crystal. I don't reply and just put my phone on the nightstand. As my thoughts fly by, I slowly fall asleep.

The rays of sun filtered by the curtains wake me. I open my eyes slowly and stand up lazily. After bathing and brushing my teeth, I put on black jeans and a turtleneck white sweater and tie my hair in a bun.

"Hello Mom," I greet mother before pressing my lips to her cheek. She smiles at me and drinks a sip of her coffee.

"Fifa, hope you slept well, darling." I nod and bite into the apple in my hand.

"Is Daddy gone?" I inquire, fishing out a bottle of apple juice from the fridge.

"Yes, he is attending a seminar in L.A."

"I'm sure you're enjoying your break," I tell her, greedily drinking my apple juice (I am an apple lover). The dark circles around her eyes are almost gone so I guess her break is making her feel better.

"Sure. Today is shopping. I don't mind going alone. I love myself enough to enjoy my own company," she gushes, making me smile.

Mother is such an amazing woman. A doctor in general practice, she is a forty-year-old, black and beautiful lady. I don't mean a random beauty, no, the Michelle Obama's kind of beauty: elegant, natural and luminous. I would have loved to tell her about what is going on inside me, but my hidden sadness closes my mouth each time I try to speak. That's because in the past it has almost destroyed everything. Once in college, I look at all the students around me. I have always thought that they live perfect lives, that they are enjoying or at least trying to prepare for a future they will relish. I can't help but only see a dark future for me. I am so frustrated about everything. While I am walking, I go over everything I planned to do on this first day of school. I am in my first year of a bachelor's in psychology; last year I was in sociology, but I changed my program.

"Fifa!" I turn to Hailey, a tall blonde girl with brown eyes. She's my friend. But I'm not sure she truly is. She hugs me warmly with a smile. She is not physically that attractive but has a charm about her.

"Hi, what's up?" I greet her with a fake warm smile.

"Guess what I did this summer…" I don't listen to her any more since I am busy remembering my notes for my philosophy class. She is always talking about herself; I don't even know if she can recall basic things about me such as my address.

"Oh baby." She kisses her boyfriend Dylan deeply, a brown, muscular boy, slightly shorter than her. Those two are kind of my only friends. I hang out with them because they are often the only ones who really accept me.

I walk in front, not minding their sweet words and public demonstration. Noticing some guy staring at me, I stop walking and frown my eyebrows, about to ask him why he was staring. The green-eyed brown boy starts walking to me with a super warm smile until he bumps into somebody. The girl curses, throwing at him an intense glare. He finally arrives in front of me — his forehead is slightly reddish, and he's massaging it with a small grin. I am taken aback on one hand by the smile because he just bumped into someone and on the other hand by the way he looks good. His lips are perfectly drawn — by the greatest architect, I could say — his face is symmetrical and his eyes... God, they are wonderful!

"Hi, you didn't answer," he says, while showing me his phone screen. I frown.

"What? Who are you?" I feel Dylan's arm wrapping round my shoulders.

"Fifa, what's up?" he asks with this showy voice I hate so much. I look back at Hailey who is talking to some girls.

"I... I am fine," is all that comes out of my mouth.

"Who's this?" he inquires looking at the boy in front of me.

"So? Why do you look so sad?" continues the boy, not minding Dylan. Oh! It's him.

"What kind of bullshit is this prat saying? She always smiles and everyone loves her," Dylan answers, sniffing my hair — awkward, I know. He always says that my hair smells like lavender.

"Can you give me a few minutes?" I ask him.

"Okay, hope you brought my things," he replies before leaving.

"So, you're that unknown who texted me? Why do you think I am sad?" I don't know why but I feel good knowing someone has noticed it.

"I just know it. So, answer me." He is looking intensely at me. He is apparently serious about his question. He doesn't mind Dylan's harsh words.

"I'm not," I blurt.

He wants to reply but Hailey grabs my wrist, ignoring him and pulling me forwards. I look back at the boy who is already talking with someone else. He gives me a quick look as I walk away from him. I don't know what he meant, but I feel like he knows me. Because through these green and deep eyes, I saw my soul.

CHAPTER TWO

A fter a few walks with the perfect annoying couple, we finally reach my faculty. I hand them Shawn Mendes' concert tickets.

"Since I could only get two, I think someone has to sacrifice themselves and you're a boy, Dylan, so..." I start explaining to them.

"I don't care. I like his songs and I want to stay with my baby," he replies while kissing her on the cheek. She lets out a weird giggle. I bite my bottom lip, aware of what is going to happen next.

"Sorry, Fifa, you wouldn't want us to be away from each other, would you?" she asks while blinking in an attempt to make me feel bad.

"All right, enjoy," I sigh.

I know it's stupid to let them manipulate me like that, but unfortunately, I always want to please everyone. I walk along the hallway to reach my class.

"Fifa, you look gorgeous this semester," a boy with a lecherous look tells me when I walk in front of him. A shiver of disgust runs through my spine when I hear his voice.

I ignore him and keep on my way, but he doesn't seem to like that. He grabs my arm and forces me to turn to him.

"I'm talking to you. We missed you so much in the football club." I finally recognize him. He is Peter, a member of the football team. As I am part of almost all the extra-curricular clubs, I found myself in their fan club. I hate that club because I am not the least interested in football. *Why then am I a member?* Because I wanted to please a girl who seemed kind to me, but she just wanted a pigeon to win the competition of the one bringing the most people. I breathe deeply and turn on him.

"What, Peter?" I say frostily, annoyed.

"I missed you," he adds. I roll my eyes.

"Well, I didn't miss you, so just leave me alone," I try to argue but he doesn't listen.

"Why do some guys like being so stupid?" We both turn to look at the boy with green eyes. He is so calm as he looks at an angry Peter.

"Are you talking to me?" Peter barks, his nostrils flare as he speaks.

"I guess, except if you are also deaf," the boy replies seriously, hands buried in his pockets. If I were him, I would just stop speaking and run away before I got beaten up. Instead of stopping them, I am too deep into watching the spectacle. Peter raises his hand to punch the other boy.

"I know you feel alone," the boy says, and Peter stops, wide-eyed.

"What?!" exclaims Peter.

"You can't argue with punches though. I have watched you several times. You should learn how to be in harmony with yourself." Both Peter and I are looking at him with wide eyes. He looks so confident.

"I think I'll go," mumbles Peter in a low voice. He walks away, staring at his feet. His face is pale as if he had seen a ghost. I don't know why but I walk fast to my class to escape the weird boy.

"Wait!" he shouts behind me, but I don't listen and walk faster. I am just thinking about one thing: getting away from him.

When I finally reach the class, I let out a breath I didn't know I was holding. *Maybe shouldn't I have run away?* I'm sure he thinks that I'm crazy because instead of thanking him, I ran away.

"Hi." I turn my head to see once more the boy from Instagram sitting by me.

"Are you some kind of psychopath?" I ask him, eyes narrowed.

"Are you, you?" he replies with a playful smile.

I can't help but smile at his bad joke. He made me smile. I can't believe it. His way of speaking freely might have caused that smile.

"Which program are you in?" I ask him to make conversation.

I don't even know his name. This encounter seems like a back-to-front way to meet someone.

"Psychology, what about you?"

"Same."

"We're going to spend time together, I guess."

I nod and turn back to my books.

I feel so stressed with all the courses. I can't mess them up, I have to succeed.

"I'm Shawn, Shawn Davis, what about you?" I lift my head up again to look at him.

"Fifame Lawson," I answer, nose in my books.

"Where are you from?"

"Benin in Africa."

It's odd that someone is so interested in my life. Shawn is a handsome tall boy with such beautiful green eyes, and he has a tattoo on the back of his left hand.

"Oh, all right," he answers.

"What was that with Peter? Were you playing the psychologist?" I ask in a low voice, glancing around. It was as if Shawn had controlled him with words. He smirks.

"I was just practicing and he was disturbing you. So, I chose to play on his weak point. He exudes a terrible loneliness despite all his supposed friends." I want to reply but the lecturer walks in.

At the end of the class, I walk out and head to the cafeteria before my second one starts. I always feel like everyone is staring at me, even when they are not. I sit quietly at a table after greeting people I know on my way, mostly from all the clubs I'm in. Seconds later, Shawn appears with his usual smile.

"How can someone like you want to be psychologist?" he inquires. I frown abruptly as a sudden anger starts growing inside me.

"What do you mean?" I snap, offended.

"I mean you look so shut up on yourself. You are not living life so why do you want to help others to live it?" he continues' less harshly.

"You don't know me," I reply, annoyed by the freedom he has to act like he knows everyone. I thought he was cool but now he is being judgmental.

"I didn't mean to offend you. I am just observing," he tries to explain; he is not even touching his food and his arms are crossed on the table.

"We just know each other since this morning," I remind him after chewing the food in my mouth.

"I've known you since your first year. I took some sociology classes first, but I chose to focus on psychology because I want to heal mentally, and I guess you did too."

"And you are not yet a psychologist so just let me breathe. Plus, you've been spying on me since last year or what?" Even though he has the name of my favorite singer, Shawn is now scaring me. I don't really know most people in my classes, so I am not surprised to not know him.

"No. I just..." He leaves his sentence hanging, probably running out of credible arguments.

I roll my eyes, grab my bag and walk out. I don't need to be around a psychopath. I don't see him in the second class. Maybe he is not in this one. Finally, I go home after a few meetings for various clubs.

When I arrive home, my mother is lying on the couch, reading a novel. She looks up at me.

"Hey sweetie, how was your first day?"

"Good," I answer briefly before going to my room.

I am used to feeling like a high school student coming back from or going to school. But since my school is not that far, the best option is to stay here. We have lived in Canada since my childhood because my father found great opportunities here and had many problems with his family in Benin. My mind is still disturbed by Shawn. I don't know why but I feel terribly guilty for being harsh to him while he was trying to be my friend. At least, I guess he wants to become my friend. I study for the rest of the day and read once again *The Interpretation of Dreams* by Freud. Maybe Shawn is right? I do know so much about psychology, but I can't apply anything to myself. As he is on my mind, I take my phone and look at his profile. He doesn't have that many followers and is mostly with friends in his photos; he always has that hope in his eyes. It is so disturbing for me. I can't help but still be confused by his beauty. I mean this boy is devilishly handsome. I find myself staring for minutes at the same pictures. I mentally slap myself for becoming obsessed – I should just forget about that weirdo boy.

My eyes fall on a picture of him: he is sticking out his tongue, his thumbs on each side of his forehead and his eyes are wide. A smile finds its way to my lips and my stomach flutters. Since when do I smile while browsing social media? I breathe deeply and finally go downstairs to have dinner with mother. Once back in bed, I try to not focus on all the bad sides of my life for once but it is quite easy because Shawn is on my mind. I am just thinking about the wise way he talks to people, the way he smiles, the way he acts like there is nothing more than what he thinks.

CHAPTER THREE

I met Dylan and Hailey a year ago. I had just joined the university and I really wanted to start over. For my senior year in high school, I had to put all my problems aside, including my best friend depression, to work and get my diploma. That was difficult, because I never wanted to see a psychologist, I never wanted to talk to anyone about what was going on inside of me, I never wanted to read pity in someone's eyes and I never wanted to burst into tears in front of any psychologist. I managed to have my parents forbid the school from letting me see any education advisor or anything close to a psychologist. At the beginning of all this, my parents didn't really trust psychologists, and still don't, but they were desperate.

Then, after my senior year of high school, I realized that I had been wrong from the beginning. I started doing research about the job that had once scared me; I wanted to understand those people who are able to read you. That year, I felt better. I realized how much we all need someone to talk to, we all have to liberate ourselves from our demons. I then wanted friends who I could trust, but no one was really there for me in school. I definitely didn't have any friends. And I didn't feel like talking about all that to my parents. That is how I decided that I wanted to help others, those people who are maybe living what I had lived. When I started college, I subscribed to all the possible clubs to make friends, but once again I was disappointed. They all just wanted to use me for what they could get and then dump me. Because my father is rich and works with many advertising companies, he gets sometimes free tickets.

One day, I was going to class when Dylan and Hailey, after kissing like two savages, called me over. I was afraid at first, but I joined them. My eyes landed on the big muscles of Dylan, his Greek nose, his large ears. Then they moved on Hailey, she was somehow simple, not beautiful, not ugly, just normal. But still, her big brown eyes were and are awesome and give her a charm.

"What's your name?" Dylan asked me like an adult talking to a child.

I answered timidly. "Fifame."

"She is cute, isn't she?" Hailey said as if I were a pet.

"Yes, she is," Dylan said before licking his bottom lip. I was disgusted and even thought that he had some perverted thoughts about me. Then I started hanging out with them, because although they used me, unlike all the others, they were always there. They were at least trying to be my friends. This is what I thought.

***

"You will find on the paper the name of your partner for this first experiment," starts the lecturer in the laboratory for the chemistry class.

The university's logo is printed on his lab coat, on the left side of his chest. The U.T was my best choice, I guess. I live in Toronto and the university is in Toronto, so I didn't have to worry too much about choosing — beside it's a great university. About this chemistry class, it's just an elective course that I've taken because I love it. As I am lost in my thoughts, I hear someone call me. It's Shawn. I blench, surprised to see him.

"Hey Fifame," he starts with his eternal smile. "You were so deep in your thoughts," he tells me with a curious look. He is too close to me; I can even feel his breath against my temple.

"Yes, are you my partner?" I ask him between two sighs.

"Yep."

"I'm sorry for yesterday. I didn't want to be mean to you," I apologize.

"Never mind, at least you expressed your emotions." He is quite right. Yesterday, I didn't feel like I had to keep how I felt to myself. Maybe because I don't know him. While we work on the experiment, he makes a few jokes. I really do love working with him.

"You will need to prepare with your partner before the next session," says the lecturer at the end. After cleaning up and submitting our work, we walk out.

"So… about the work, we can do it this Saturday if you don't mind," I start whilst we are walking to the cafeteria.

"Sure, you can come to my place," he responds.

I feel secretly relieved that we will work at his place. I don't really want my mother to ask him weird questions. We reach the cafeteria and sit at an empty table.

"SpongeBob is far one of the best cartoons, I swear." He laughs after telling me about the episode he loved the best: the one about the magic cove. We are both a bit immature in our taste for cartoons and I find his description entertaining.

"I think, I prefer 'Tom and Jerry'," I reply remembering some episodes of that crazy cartoon.

"Who doesn't like that?" he asks while shrugging.

"'Tom and Jerry', I guess. It shouldn't be funny to be fighting all the time," I reply and smile at my bad joke.

"Yeah, but... "

"Darling!" I lift my head up to see Hailey and Dylan, showing up at the wrong time as always.

"Hey," I answer awkwardly.

"Hello," says Shawn, smiling to them. They ignore him.

"Fifa, you should come and eat with us," says Dylan.

"But we never do. You guys said I must let you enjoy your relationship," I protest.

"Come on, get up. We miss you."

I look at Shawn who is not smiling any more, his gaze glued on me. I don't know what to do. I don't know if Shawn will be permanent in my life, but I know they have been there since last year. They are still my friends. I stand up with my food and follow them to their table.

"Bye," I smile to Shawn, but he doesn't look at me. There are a few other guys who I don't know, left at the table. Someone sits next to Shawn. They are already talking and laughing. I feel guilty for leaving him and a little jealous that he makes someone else laugh too. Dylan and Hailey are ignoring me now. I don't get why they called me over to live in their perfect world. My eyes are focused on Shawn, on how his chest shakes when he laughs, on how he runs his tongue over his lips, on...

"Fifa, did you hear me?"

I blench and look at the guy by me.

"Wh... What?" I stammer. The tips of his blonde hair are tinted red, a little cream is spread on his nose; I am not good at remembering people's names.

"Can you come around to help me clean? We're going to have a party soon."

"Sure." I don't know him or which party he is talking about but I don't mind. I am sometimes tired from doing this for everyone when they don't care about my life at all. I look again at Shawn, but he is not there any more. I don't see him much more during the day except in class, and he is less talkative. When I get home, the house is empty. I make myself dinner and text Shawn.

Hi! I am so sorry about what happened.

He doesn't reply even though I can see he's online. I am afraid I have lost the only real friend I was starting to have. The dark thoughts take over me for the whole night again. My anxiety is growing now that I feel like I've ruined everything with him. He barely talks to me the rest of the week. I am back to my sad life: people telling me what to do and me just doing that and nothing for myself. Shawn is right. How can I expect to help people if I can't even help myself? Friday evening, I stay at home as usual. I don't really like parties. I study to try to forget everything else. My phone beeps and I jump on it.

Hey. Meet me at my house at 2 pm. This is my address XXX.

My chest hurts when I read his message. He is really angry if he just texts for that. I just hope that tomorrow will not be a bad day.

"What's wrong, Fifa?" my mom asks me during dinner. Since the worse of my depression ended, this is the first time I haven't managed to control these bad feelings and have shown them.

"Nothing, just tired," I answer.

"It's normal. You've taken on responsibility for too much," she complains.

"I haven't'."

"You have. Listen, you should slow down and enjoy your life."

15

"I will, Mom. Thanks." I don't want to extend the conversation. I just give her a fake smile and concentrate on my food. I feel like I might crack at any time and burst into tears and I don't want to.

Saturday, I can't stop thinking about Shawn and our meeting this afternoon. A ball squeezes in my stomach when I think about how bad it could get. Around one, I start getting ready. I try almost all the clothes in my closet and nothing seems to fit me. I am so frustrated. I finally decide to just dress casually: jeans and a top with my favorite brown cardigan and black boots. He doesn't live that far from me. The house is pretty nice. I park the car and walk to the door. I press the bell. I am so stressed and my hands are shaking. Seconds later, he opens the door, wearing just shorts. My eyes stop on his torso. I blush and a heat starts growing in my stomach. His eyes are sleepy as if he just woke up. I am just praying for everything to go well.

CHAPTER FOUR

The wind is tugging at my hair which resists painfully in its bun. My eyes blink awkwardly while flicking between Shawn's chest and his face which is even more beautiful on waking. *Stop Fifa*, my consciousness warns me. He looks surprised to see me and runs his hand through his hair.

"Oh, Fifa. Sorry, I forgot you were coming. I can easily get distracted," he apologizes while scratching his temple.

"Never mind, I could have answered when you gave me the address yesterday," I tell him, talking both about me answering him and him answering me.

"Come in."

I walk in, looking around. The inside is very nice and well cared for. The interior opens onto a small lobby like ours but with Turkish rugs while ours is decorated with African fabric ones. There are flowers everywhere which gives a natural charm to the house. I am relieved he is not mad or at least, he is not showing it.

"You can wait here. I will make us some snacks and wear a T-shirt, I guess," he says and smiles to me. We are in the living room. The TV is on and a funny movie is playing. My eyes land on an old woman on the couch; she is staring at the screen.

"Grandma, my friend is here. We are going to work," he tells her softly before walking out.

His friend? We are friends?

"A friend?" she says while looking around like she can't see me. "Come and sit by me. I know you are a girl, I can smell your nice perfume." I sit near her and she turns to me. She has a nice scent, a motherly scent. My gaze lingers on the horizontal rhythmic movements of her eyeballs and her vague gaze. I feel a sudden lump in my throat, she is blind. She gently puts her soft hands on mine while smiling.

"You are his girlfriend, aren't you?"

I blush. "No... um. We are... friends," I correct her, looking away, quite overreacting.

"Oh sorry, I thought he was just hiding it from me. He was so excited about you coming here." I am secretly thrilled by this.

"You are watching a movie...? I mean listening... I mean..." I mentally slap myself for being so clueless. Building a sentence shouldn't be that difficult.

"Calm down sweetie. Yeah, I am listening. Our favorite movies, Shawn's and mine, are the funny ones. You should come one day for a movie night." Her revelation about Shawn's kind of movie choice doesn't surprise me.

"Sounds good."

"What's your name?"

I really like that genuine interest in her voice, it feels like she cares.'

"Fifame."

"Nice. I know Benin very well. You can call me Frida."

"Hey, we can go."

I lift my head up to Shawn with some snacks in his hands. I gently squeeze Frida's hands and smile to her even though she can't see me.

"See you." She smiles back to me and turns back to her movie.

We walk into a large room with pictures everywhere. Some of Shawn and Frida together. Those two are special: on one of the photos, they are wearing tango outfits, their tongues are out and they are pulling silly faces while Shawn holds Frida in his arms. "She absolutely wanted me to learn tango and all the possible dances. Also, she wants me to know about many cultures because she travelled all over the world," Shawn tells me as my eyes are moving over the pictures. But on many of the pictures, we can see people smiling with Shawn at their side. "I've kind of volunteered with lots of charities," he tells me as my eyes are glued to the picture on which a little girl is kissing him on the cheek. She has stars in her eyes, hopeful and dreamy stars, the sort we could never lose.

However, those stars are the sort dying in thousands of children's eyes all over the world. Once, Michelle Obama said "There are not bad children, but bad circumstances." I totally believe in her words, bad circumstances stole the stars in my eyes, years ago. My eyes finally land on Shawn who has put a shirt on — I secretly would rather he hadn't.

"Have a seat," he tells me, showing me a table. I do as asked, and he follows suit.

"Before we start, I want to apologize again for leaving you that time," I start, nervously wringing my fingers.

"Uh, never mind. I was disappointed but it's in the past. And I guess they are your friends?" The last sentence sounds more like a question. A question I also ask myself. I smile to him and we get down to work for about three hours.

By the time we are done, it is five. He stretches and puts his hand back on the table. I notice his tattoo once again. "What is the meaning?" I ask him while staring at his tattoo. His eyes land on it and he smiles. Dimples dig into his cheeks when he smiles, making him even more adorable. I have a weakness for dimples, I admit it. I know I wouldn't ever get tired of his smile.

"It's called the evil, even though it doesn't have anything to do with it. See, it looks like the symbol for infinity, but with an arrow. It means you have to experience setbacks and problems in order to move forward," he explains to me while passing his index finger over the tattoo. My gaze is focused on him, trying to understand who Shawn is.

"Why do you look so... happy?" I inquire shyly. He looks at me, I still can't look him straight in the eye, his are so deep.

"I will answer if you answer my previous question."

"I... I don't know what you meant," I lie.

"Yes, you do," he replies looking once more into my eyes. I don't know why my heart suddenly starts racing, like those fast cars in the movies, without any chance of stopping. He gently puts his hand on mine. Shivers run through my skin. He says so softly, "Are you always sad?"

My eyes are focused on the small circles he is drawing on the back of my hand and my breathing slows down.

"Yes. Every night," I answer honestly through a sigh. This is the first time I've opened myself to someone. I feel all the emotions running in my heart and I can't meet his eyes any more. I don't know how to explain everything that happens to me; I don't know if anyone would understand that I will never get over my depression. I don't know if anyone can just get why I act like everything is all right while I cry almost every night.

"Do you want me to tell you a secret?" he replies, pulling me from my bad thoughts. I nod. "Happiness is a choice," he says softly. I look at him, frowning. I am lost in his eyes; I can feel heat rising in me.

"Where are your parents? I'm sure your whole family is like you," I try to joke.

"My parents are dead. They died few years ago," he answers with a hint of sadness.

"Oh… sorry." I feel so bad for him. I don't know what I would do if my parents died. I know one day they will, but I am just not ready for it.

"Don't worry. I am good with Grandma. Even though with her disease, it's not always easy."

"Which disease?" my curiosity pushes me to ask.

"She has a kind of brain disease. That's why she is blind. Sometimes she is there physically, but she is not really there." I feel the sadness in his voice even though he is trying to hide it. He sighs. "This conversation is getting heavy, isn't it? What are you planning to do for the rest of the day?" he inquires, crossing his arms on the table. I almost miss his hand on mine.

"Well, I really wanted to go to the Shawn Mendes' concert but my friends took the tickets from me." Coming out of my mouth, that sounds awkward and stupid. Friends would never act like Dylan and Hailey act with me.

"You really want to go?" he asks me. I am taken aback by his question, but I nod. "Give me five minutes." He stands and takes his laptop.

Minutes later, he prints something and comes back with two tickets for the concert. "I bought them from someone. Much more expensive but it doesn't matter."

"Oh. You shouldn't have done that. I mean, the concert starts in less than an hour and it was sold out. That's too much."

"Happiness doesn't have price," he answers simply.

He goes to the bathroom and comes back in jeans and a black t-shirt.

"We are going out. Just do what I told you if you need me," he explains gently to Frida, crouched in front of her and stroking gently her cheek.

"Well. Take care of yourselves," she replies before he kisses her on the forehead.

We finally leave the house. "I came with my car," I tell him once we are outside.

"We can go with mine and when we get back, you'll take yours."

I nod. As he is driving, I catch myself staring at him. He also catches me and smiles to me, and I blush.

"What?"

"Nothing. Just, I can't believe I actually met someone like you," I tell him with a grin.

"Someone like me?" he asks, surprised.

"Yeah. I mean you're so… perfect," I blush again and turn my head to the window to observe the landscape and so I don't have to face his look.

"I'm not." He smiles again. His face must ache, smiling so much.

"Can you imagine that you are going to Shawn's concert with Shawn? You are lucky girl."

I chuckle. The line for the concert is very long. I see Dylan, Hailey and two other guys with them. They are walking towards our side. I pray they don't see us.

"Fifa?" Hailey's voice is full of surprise as she calls to me. I turn to her with a small smile. "I didn't know you were coming."

"Nor me," I answer glancing at Shawn.

"Hi Fifa, thanks for the tickets," the short brown skin boy following them tells me.

"Which ones?" I ask, frowning.

"The ones you gave Dylan for us."

My eyes pain me. I want to cry. They are smiling at me like it's normal. I regain control of myself and give a humorless smile. "You are welcome. Enjoy." This is the only thing I can say.

"And... you got a new friend?" Hailey asks, looking at Shawn. I don't exactly know how I am feeling actually. I know Hailey and Dylan are just friends with me for their own benefit but I would never imagine they would act like this, taking gifts from me and hanging out with everyone but me, taking me for a stupid girl. Maybe I am that stupid girl.

"I..." I finally start to say but she waves her hand.

"Never mind. Take care," she continues, and they leave. Shawn gently squeezes my hand. I don't know what is going on. I don't know how they think of me while I am stupidly taking them as friends. This hits me even more now.

CHAPTER FIVE

I turn to Shawn who looks at me, worry filling his eyes. "I don't know why you hang out with them. You deserve better," he tells me.

"They are kind of my only friends since I came here." I try, more to convince myself than him.

"I don't call that friends," he asserts and gestures after them with his chin. The concert helps me to relax after the treachery of my so-called friends. Shawn was so great, he always is. Both Shawns were-Mendes and Davis. After the concert, it is past ten.

"I'm hungry. Are you?" he asks me as he pulls out of the parking lot.

"Yes, very," I groan, holding my stomach as if I haven't eaten for days.

"Let's get something to eat."

He puts on some gospel music. I am surprised he likes that kind of music. A Jonathan Nelson song fills the car; the melody is calm and transports us to another universe. We both sing as we drive along. We enter the restaurant. It looks like one of those family restaurants: nice and simple. A chef walks towards us with a smile.

"*Mama mia!* Our boy Shawn is here with a delicious girl," he says as he squeezes Shawn's hand and hugs me with a kiss on each cheek. He has a round tummy and a mustache. A slim woman, also a chef, walks to us seconds later. She is blonde and very fine.

"So nice to see you, *bambini,*" she says, hugging both of us.

They have Italian accents. There are people eating and talking in the restaurant. I like the atmosphere here: it is familiar and pleasant.

"Come and sit," the woman says as she pulls us towards a table in the corner.

Before we sit, Shawn finally speaks, "Fifa these are old friends of my parents. Alicio and his wife Alessia. They are great people. Alicio and Alessia, this is my friend Fifame, the greatest girl I know actually." I blush and smile at them.

"Nice to meet you *bellissima*," they both say before hugging me again.

"Me too," I reply shyly.

When we are finally sitting, Shawn says appreciatively, "You will soon taste the best pizza of your life." I smile. "I love coming here. I feel like I'm at home," he tells me and I look around once again.

"It is my first time, but I already love it," I reply, still admiring the homey place. The pizza finally comes and my mouth waters as soon as my eyes land on the food and the smell fills my nostrils. My stomach claps hands, ready to taste a culinary marvel.

"Enjoy your meal," he wishes me, looking at me the way he does since we met and that makes me melt.

"Same to you."

We eat while talking.

"What do Italians ghost eat for dinner?" I have food in my mouth, so I chew quickly, shrugging. "Spook-getti," he whispers as if it were a secret and I almost spit my food out. The joke is not actually so funny, but he makes it so special.

"You are crazy, Shawn," I tell him and chuckle.

"Well, everyone is either crazy or normal. And normal people are boring," he replies before sticking out his tongue at me like a child. A smile finds a way to my lips. I have never smiled this much in my life without trying to hide bad feelings behind it. After dinner we say goodbye to Alicio and Alessia and go back to Shawn's.

"I really enjoyed this day," he says when we are in front of the house. He is leaning against his car and I am just in front of him. He is so tall, especially for the short person that I am.

"You look like a little doll," he teases me.

I roll my eyes. "I don't," I protest before crossing my arms and pouting.

"Come on. Now you look like those adorable pets. Do you want to kill people "with your stunning good looks?" My cheeks turn red and I look away. I give him a gentle slap on the arm.

"You are crazy."

"I know, you told me earlier," he says in a soft tone before smiling. Butterflies are fluttering joyfully in my stomach. I can't help but feel so good with him.

"I should come in and say goodbye to Frida," I tell him looking at the house.

"Don't worry, she'll be asleep at this time," he says, checking his watch.

"Oh, all right. So... goodbye?"

We look awkwardly at each other. I go up on tiptoe to hug him; he hugs me back. It lasts for some minutes. We are hugging each other so hard that it looks like we can't let go. His scent tickles my nostrils. He smells good. We finally separate from each other and walk to my car. I get in and he closes the door like a gentleman, a sexy, beautiful gentleman. He waves; I am not sure but feel like he doesn't want me to leave. When I finally get home, it's past eleven. My mother is slumped on the couch, watching an episode of *One Piece*. She does like anime, even more than I do. I love her so much; I love her for those small details that make her the wonderful mother she is. She looks up at me as soon as I close the door.

"This is the first time you've come home late," she notes but there is no reprimand in her voice. I turn nineteen next week so she doesn't really have much to say. I respect my parents and I am a kind of a model daughter.

"Yes. I was with... a friend," I tell her, embarrassed and bite my top lip at the last word.

"That friend makes you blush. I want to meet him... or her?"

I roll my eyes and walk quickly to my room. "Goodnight Mommy."

"Goodnight darling."

I take a quick shower and pull on my Dragon Ball Z pajamas. I am kind of a manga lover; did I mention that? I lie down and start looking at Shawn's pictures online. I still wonder what I did to deserve someone like him. He came into my life just a week ago and I already feel like I am a new person. When I leave his profile, my eyes land on a picture of Dylan, Hailey and their two friends at the concert. I can't stop thinking about all I have done to please them, to be their friend but they are still disrespecting me.

Don't think about the shitty friends you have, because now you have me.

I smile while reading this nice text from Shawn. He also sends me a few jokes better than the previous ones he told me. Then he calls me. I pick up without hesitation.

"You miss me that much?" I tease him, picking at my nails, a huge excited grin on my face.

"I just felt like you do," he replies; I can picture him smiling playfully right now.

"I love the jokes, by the way," I tell him, remembering the one I liked best.

"That was the point. I'm sorry for what they did to you. You should dump them."

"Dump them?" I repeat while moving all around the room. I can't stay at one place.

"Definitely. I just wanted to hear your voice before sleeping," he admits, and I blush. *Yes, again.* "I guess you are blushing," he adds.

"I'm not," I assert.

"I'm sure you are, you always are. But it's cute."

"What are you doing tomorrow?" I inquire, watching the stars through my window.

"I will work and watch movies with Grandma, I guess."

"Don't you want to know what I will do?" I ask him in a baby voice.

"No, I don't care," he teases me.

I roll my eyes but still amused by his teasing mood. "Well, I'm also going to work, then I will go shopping with Mom and then play it by ear."

"So exciting!" he teases me again and we both laugh.

"Goodnight Fifa," he finally says after a few more minutes.

"Goodnight Shawn. May God protect you."

We hang up. I actually sleep well, very well. I dream about Shawn. My savior, my remedy.

CHAPTER SIX

S unday is calm. Shawn texts me in the morning to wish me a nice day, so I text him the same. In the evening, I help my mother to cook before father comes back from L.A. I am smiling and singing "Treat You Better" by Shawn Mendes while setting the table. I notice that Mom's staring at me and I frown.

"What's wrong?" I ask her.

"Nothing, I just like the way you are today. You were cool when we went shopping too," she says meaningfully, pouring water into her glass. She can't drink alcohol as she is on call tonight.

"I always am." She rolls her eyes and smiles at me. When we are finally done setting the table, the doorbell rings.

"I'll go." I walk to the door, open it to my father and help him with his bags. "Welcome home, Dad," I say and hug him. He looks surprised but doesn't reply. This is the first time I've given him a hug in a long time. He waves to Mom and we have dinner. I sometimes wonder if they really love each other. They behave more like friends than lovers.

I wake up in a good mood on Monday, ready for the new week.

Happiness tip one: Always relax and take it slow.

I don't reply to Shawn's message and get ready for school. During the philosophy class, the lecturer asks for our assignments. I spent a long time on mine and I am entirely proud of the result. I look into my bag, but

I don't see my work. My heart stops beating and my hand shakes. No! I put the bag on the table and search all through it hoping for a miracle.

"What's wrong?" Shawn asks me while I am consumed with fear.

"My work, I didn't bring it," I sigh.

"What was tip one?" he asks me too calmly.

"It's not the moment, Shawn," I whine, annoyed.

"Answer."

"Always check you've got your work?" I tease him, glancing at my bag one last time. He rolls his eyes.

"Keep calm. Don't kill yourself for an assignment," he says as if it was so simple.

"I'm going to get a big zero and I don't actually want it," I panic.

"Fifa, just please trust me for once," he begs me.

"So, what do you suggest?" The lecturer had gone out to talk with someone so we can talk without disturbing anyone.

"Just wait for the end and tell him," he proposes, his elbow on the table.

I raise an eyebrow. "That's your solution?"

"Sure."

I sigh but trust him. I watch all the students stand up to give in their work. I frantically jiggle my legs and tap the bench with my fingers. Shawn has an amused smile on his lips. "Can't you stop moving so much?" he teases me after coming back from the front. I shoot him a dirty look that he smirks at. "What's the nickname of a pressure cooker?" I give him a side look that says, "Like seriously?" but it doesn't stop him from saying, "Fifame cooker." Then he smirks again. I am planning on revenge.

At the end, Shawn follows me to see the lecturer. I am so nervous and my head is lowered.

"Can I talk to you, please?" I ask the lecturer.

"Sure, can I help you?" Shawn moves his hand slowly up and down on my back to support me.

"I... I'm so sorry, I forgot my work and I swear I did it." I chew on my bottom lip, nervous.

"Don't worry, bring it to Wednesday's class. But be more careful in the future."

"I promise," I tell him, kissing my fingers, like the Latinos do in their movies, to swear. He smiles to me and we leave the class.

"Look, it was not that difficult in the end."

"Yes, thank you."

"You're welcome."

We walk to the cafeteria. We pass Dylan and Hailey but they ignore us. I think it is better like that.

"Why are you part of all the clubs. Do you love all those activities?" Shawn asks me, eyes narrowed. He looks so adorable I could eat him like a candy.

"Actually no. But..."

"Which ones do you really like?" He doesn't let me finish.

"Well, it hasn't started yet, but I do love the O.V. (Orphans Voice) club. I really love the fact that they write letters to the orphans, to share love with them. They organize all those activities for them," I babble with admiration. This kind of club isn't part of a bigger network, some students at the college just decided to create it.

"Then you should just go there. Just do what you love. It's even the only club I am part of," he tells me before drinking his Diet Coke.

***

Today is my birthday. I am officially nineteen. I thank all those unknown people on the internet and those I barely talk to for their birthday messages. I don't have any message from Shawn. I tell myself that he will maybe tell me happy birthday when I see him.

"My baby is nineteen," Mom welcomes me when I enter the kitchen. She kisses me emotionally and my father also gives me a kiss. We can be a kissing family.

"It's just a birthday," I remind them. But a big smile is shining on my face.

"Not just a birthday. I can't believe my baby is a woman." She is crying.

"Happy birthday," they finally say together.

"Thank you." I smile at them. After a fun breakfast with Mom recalling the most awkward moments of my childhood, I make my way to U.T. It's Friday and I don't have that many classes. I park my car in the school parking lot and walk to my faculty. To accompany my brown leggings, I am wearing a yellow sweatshirt on which it's written "Black and Yellow". Someone told me once that black girls look nice in yellow. Even though I am not fully black but more, brown skinned, I think he is right. Father has very fair skin because his mother is from France and his father is from Benin. They both live in Benin though. Almost all the people from the different clubs have forgotten my birthday but I don't bother to remind them. Those who do remember wish me happy birthday either with a fake enthusiasm or nonchalantly. I meet Dylan and Hailey.

"Sweetie, long time no see," Hailey starts. Seems like they don't want to ignore me today.

"Yep. Aren't you with your friend today?" Dylan asks, looking around to check Shawn is not hidden anywhere. A red bandana is around his head, on the front, it's written f*ck bitches. This boy is so vulgar.

"No," I sigh. I was expecting them to at least remember my birthday, but they don't.

"Is there a problem?" Hailey asks me, wrinkling her nose.

"No, no."

I still haven't heard from Shawn by the evening and I start to worry. What if something's happened to him? What if he just doesn't want to see me any more? I try to call him several times, but he doesn't pick up nor answer my texts. What if he has been tricking me all this time? I can't imagine him doing that; he is not like that. I am closed in my room, deep in my thoughts, imagining all the possible scenarios.

"Fifa, you have a visitor," my mother tells me from downstairs. Does anyone I know ever come here? No one knows where I live. Hailey and Dylan came here once but I can bet they don't remember the address. I join my mother in the living room. Three pairs of eyes are staring at me as my eyes are focus on just one person. What happened?

CHAPTER SEVEN

S hawn is in front of me. His eyes are bloodshot, his hair is messy and he looks exhausted. He has dark circles under his eyes. I can't help but throw my arms around him.

"Shawn!" He hugs me back. When I notice that my parents are staring at us, I pull away from him and clear my throat. "Hi!"

"Hey," he answers.

"Mom, Dad, it's my... friend Shawn." They are looking at us with weird smiles. "I think we need to head to my room," I chuckle, amused by what I anticipate will be Dad's reaction.

"You what?" My father stands up, but my mother covers his mouth with her hand. I pull Shawn quickly away before he notices how crazy my parents are. We enter the room.

"Your parents are nice," he says as we sit on the bench by the big window.

"I guess."

"Happy birthday," he smiles and hands me a small box.

"Thank you." I say while opening the box. It is a silver necklace with the letter F. It is very pretty and charming. "Oh, so nice, thank you."

"I know it's weird actually. But I just wanted to show you with this, that I will always be there for you. I just appeared out of nowhere, this strange person, but you are really important to me," he admits.

"You didn't have to get me anything but thank you. Tell me, how did you get here?" I ask him, putting the small box on my desk.

"GPS. Your location is on Instagram."

"I really should come off social media," I remark.

"I'm sorry I couldn't tell you happy birthday earlier. Grandma was ill last night, and my phone has been at home all day. When we got home, I just took it and looked for your house," he explains to me.

"What's wrong with her? Is she okay?" I start to worry.

"Yes, she is," he answers but I feel like he is hiding things from me.

"I thought you forgot about my birthday," I confess to him, my eyes lowered.

"I guess your fake friends did," he says with a sympathetic smile.

"Actually, yes," I admit, ashamed. He puts his hand on mine and squeezes it gently.

"I'm not them," he whispers. My eyes are buried in his and my heart is beating too fast. We stare out at the stars, in silence. At least, until I break it.

"Why me? Why are you so perfect with me?" I had to ask him. All this seems like a dream; Shawn is a dream. He can't be real.

"Because you deserve it. No one should think anything is too good for them," he whispers.

I smile. "Help me to put it on," I finally say and grab the box. He opens it. I turn my back to him. As he touches my skin, shivers run down my spine. I stand up to look at myself in the mirror. The letter rests on my chest and the necklace is shining on my skin. "It's perfect," I whisper with a smile. I feel his eyes on me, and I can hardly focus on my reflection. I sit back beside him after admiring my gift for a long while.

"What did you do today?" he finally asks.

"Just routine stuff. "

"On your birthday?" he says with surprise.

"Yes. There is not that much to do," I remind him and shrug.

"Tomorrow, I will put this right," he says finally.

"You really don't have to do all this for me," I remind him.

"I just want to, so let me do what I want," he replies. "Can I ask you a question?" I frown slightly but nod. "Will you go back to your sadness when I'm not there?" My chest hurts as the words leave his mouth. My eyes are already watering. I don't want him to leave me one day, I need him.

"You... Why are you asking that question?" I look at him, worried.

"I'm not going to leave you, don't worry." He takes my hand in his. "I mean, when I am not around, you go back to your sadness, don't you?"

I look down and confess, "Yes."

"You don't need anyone to be happy. You have to be happy with yourself, do you know that?"

"I guess," I sigh. He lifts up my chin for me to look at him. I don't know why I always shiver when he touches me.

"But that doesn't mean that you have to just stay by yourself. You should learn to be happy whether you are hanging out alone or with people." I know he is right but the only people I've given my trust to have betrayed me. Since my childhood it has been the same thing.

"I think I'm broken," I whisper between my teeth, looking away. I don't want to unlock that box. I don't want to remember things.

"What do you mean?" he asks curiously.

"I... I don't know. Please, I don't want to talk about this," I have started to cry. All my body is trembling as the memories shake my brain. I don't want to remember.

"Oh... don't cry. It's your birthday." He brushes the tears from my cheeks with his thumbs. "We will talk about it later." I look back at him, frowning. "Yes, we will. You will reopen those old wounds and we will heal them together," he tells me slowly before kissing me on the forehead. He touches my cheek softly, drawing small circles. His head is too close; I can feel his breath against my face, the heat of his body. I can feel my soul connecting with his, the night meeting the day, the light taking over the dark. Someone knocks at the door, making me jump. I stand up quickly and clean my wet cheeks.

"We are going to have dinner, darling," my mom says behind the door.

"We are coming downstairs," I tell her loudly. I turn to Shawn who is walking to me. My eyes are staring at his lips. "I would like you to join us."

"No one says no to food." We both smile.

"He is going to have dinner with us," I say as we enter the kitchen.

"Great. That will be lovely. I made a specialty from Benin. You will love it." My mother looks down, she stares at our intertwined fingers. I quickly remove my hand while my eyes meet the angry ones of my father. He is not used to seeing a boy around me. We all look awkwardly at one another. I help mom to set the table. We all sit and take each other's hands to pray, eyes closed.

"Dear God, bless this food and our family," Mom starts.
"Feed all the hungry people in the world," I continue.
"And bless all the humans in the world," Father finishes.
"Amen," we all say, including Shawn.

"Do you live with your parents or alone?" my mother asks Shawn during the dinner. I knew she would bombard him with questions. Nosy woman.

"No, I don't live with them," he says with a small smile.

"Don't you miss them? I am so happy my daughter is still living here." I warn her with my eyes but she doesn't mind me.

"Mom, I think you should let him eat," I warn her again.

"My parents are dead. I live with my grandma," he finally says with a look that says, "Don't worry, it's fine".

"Oh sorry. You should come around for dinner sometimes and bring her," Mom tries make amends.

"Sure." I admire this boy so much; he is so special.

"And what are you studying in college? Isn't it difficult with the school fees? If you need any help you can count on us." I look at my father, surprised. He seems to like him now.

"I'm studying psychology. Thank you, but I started university with my student savings account, and now I have a scholarship. And besides my grandma has savings and I work too."

"You are brilliant then. Fifa also has a scholarship. I am glad she has a friend like her. Not like those two parasites."

He adds some garri on his rice before adding the sauce. Gari is a semolina of cassava. Most Beninese travel with it, and father orders it regularly. I love it because you can add it to anything or eat it alone or with water or even make a dish like Eba out of it.

41

"Dad!" I know Shawn is holding himself from laughing but he is smiling, like my mother. I know he agrees with my father about Dylan and Hailey.

"I just do my best for my parents to be proud of me from heaven. By the way the food is really tasty Mrs Lawson," he says in a calm tone. I must be looking at him with stars in the eyes.

At the end of the dinner, my mother puts the cake on the table. She has made a strawberry cake with chocolate biscuits. We all stand next to it. They sing happy birthday to me. I feel happy.

"Make a wish," Dad says to me. I look at them, smile and make a wish: I want everyone in the world to find this happiness. We eat the delicious cake, joke and laugh.

"Goodbye. You're a sweet boy," my mother says while hugging Shawn. She even pats his head. Father and he shake hands.

"Son, you have my respect," my father says to him. I have never seen him showing any affection to anyone but mother and me. I guess it is a time for change. I walk Shawn to the door and close it behind me.

"Happy birthday again," he says to me. We are standing and it's pretty cold despite the fact that it's autumn. I feel like it is always cold in Canada. I adjust my jacket around my body. Shawn's nose is red and I can see that he is cold.

"Thanks." He hugs me; we always hug each other hard. I love feeling his arms around me, knowing that he is there for me, smelling his gorgeous scent. I find my lips against his. It feels so good. My lips are dancing softly with his. The heat rises inside of me. The whole universe hovers around me and butterflies are dancing in my stomach. He puts his hands on the sides of my head. His tongue waltzes with mine. Those lips I have always stared at are now on mine. When we finally separate, we smile to each other. No word is necessary.

"Goodnight," he whispers.

"Goodnight."

I stay in front of the house, my mind flying, watching him get into his car. He smiles to me and leaves. This is my best birthday so far.

CHAPTER EIGHT

When I go to bed my heart is light. The kiss with Shawn remains etched in my memory, like a beautiful scar that stays on your skin forever. I take my phone and text him to let me know when he gets home. Then I bite my bottom lip and pull the blanket over my body. Someone knocks at the door; I quickly glance at it. "Come in." My mother enters with a wistful smile and sits next to me on the bed. She takes my hand in hers. She looks so emotional.

"Is anything wrong, Mom?" I sit up, looking at her, puzzled.

"Nothing, darling. I just missed seeing you happy." My heart gets heavier the more I watch her bright eyes.

"I have always been," I lie.

"You know mothers, we feel things, and some nights, I hear you cry alone in your room." Her revelation burns my heart. I painfully swallow the excess of saliva in my mouth. "I was so worried about seeing you depressed again. Especially on those days you didn't eat at all. Since that day you came home from elementary school, I knew something had happened to you. But you were so shut up on yourself that I could never know what it was. I'm so glad you met that boy. I feel like he is healing you. I have been powerless all this time."

She is crying and I am too. All that time, I thought no one was seeing my sadness; I thought no one cared enough to see it and that no one would ever see it. I thought I had the right to be depressed. And, paradoxically, I thought I didn't have the right to be depressed. Because lots of people are suffering much more in this life, because so many people are enduring worse things. While me, I had a good life and a perfect family. I just didn't have the right, and I felt guilty. Now I just realize that I have the right to be sad but not to stay sad. I could have just opened myself up. Just spoken. But depression didn't want me to. I hug my mother tightly. I feel how much she loves me, how much she doesn't want me to suffer. When she finally leaves, I take the big box from under my bed. I look at the photos inside it. Some are photos of me, so happy, before that day. I was a quirky little girl, mixing clothes and styles. For one Halloween, I was dressed as both Hermione from Harry Potter and Ludmila from Violetta: yes, that is a weird mixture. For another one, I made a monster costume with Mom and we added some princess stuff. That year, I won the fancy dress contest at school. The other kids were extremely mad. Some of the pictures were taken since that day, when I started losing too much weight, when I was deep in my depression. Fortunately, I have this great family.

I'm back home. Goodnight sweetie.

I smile at his text and reply.

Goodnight Shawn.

***

The ringtone of my phone wakes me up. I groan but reach for it slowly. It's four a.m. and Shawn is calling.

"What's wrong?" I ask him as soon as I pick up. My voice is hoarse, and my eyes are too heavy to stay open.

"I'm in front of your house, put on your sport clothes and get down," he orders and hangs up. As soon as he hangs up, I fall back asleep. But he calls me again. An irrepressible desire to murder goes through my body but I get hold of myself and stand up, brush my teeth and get dressed. When I walk out of the house, I see Shawn leaning against his car, headphones in his ears. A smile that slides onto my lips kills my previous desire to kill him. I walk towards him; he turns his head to me and smiles.

"Sport is the best way to alleviate stress," he tells me as soon as I reach him.

"Did you need to wake me up that early?" I half joke.

"Yes, I guess," he says playfully, and I roll my eyes.

We jog, each of us immersed in the music that fills our ears. He is very speedy, as quick as a mouse (I think they are extremely fast). As I am not used to this, it is difficult to keep it up. Despite all my muscles crying and begging, I gather all my strength to run faster. He looks back at me and smiles playfully, then runs faster still. I try to keep up but I stumble and fall. Fortunately, the streets are empty. I frown, still on the floor and Shawn turns to me and bursts out laughing. He holds his tummy and I can even see him wipe a tear from the corner of his eye. Then, he walks to me and gives me his hand, still laughing. I pull him down and he falls and I burst out laughing too. So, we are sitting on the sidewalk, laughing like two crazy people. Maybe are we crazy. We finally get back home around six. I stop, breathing noisily, hands on my hips.

"I could have died, you know."

He chuckles and replies, "But you didn't. Stay positive. Don't you feel better?" We walk inside. I feel really good; my body is relaxed and even my mind is lighter.

"Yes." We stand in the kitchen and I pour two glasses of lemon water. He drinks his in one go.

"Why did the lemon stop rolling down the hill?" Instant joke, I guess, and wait for him to answer. "It ran out of juice," he adds playfully. I burst out laughing and he follows suit.

"Where do you find all your jokes?" I finally ask.

"Internet," he confesses and it makes me laugh harder. "But I can make some up if you want me to," he adds with a seductive smile and walks over to me.

"I'm sure you're bad," I say with difficulty, because my back is glued to the counter and Shawn has his hands on each side of my body. His eyes are immersed in mine.

"I guess so." His deep, sensual voice makes me shiver and his eyes staring at my lips make me dizzy. He lowers his head to kiss me.

"Oh my God!" We both jump and separate, blushing furiously. My mom had her hand against her mouth, but she is now smiling playfully.

"I guess some are spending a nice Saturday," she sings.

"Good morning, Mrs Lawson," Shawn stammers, extremely embarrassed.

"Hello Shawn. I don't have any problem with lovers but I don't think George would like to see your tongue in his daughter's mouth in his kitchen," my mother jokes, making us blush more.

"Sorry," he says, looking away.

"Never mind," she smiles to him. Mother has a talent for embarrassing people. Shawn clears his throat and looks at me.

"I am leaving. See you later," he tells me.

"Let me escort you."

He says goodbye to my mother, and we walk to the door. We both chuckle on the way. He turns to me.

"I don't want to die this young so..." He kisses me on the cheek. "Bye Fifa." Then he leaves. I know I am going to see him again this evening but I can't help but miss him. I walk back inside and my mother looks at me knowingly. I just roll my eyes while walking to my room to take a shower.

CHAPTER NINE

I put on a black dress that comes down to mid-thigh and a pair of tights. My frizzy hair is tied in a bun on top of my head and I choose to wear light makeup. I go downstairs to open the door to Shawn who has just rung the bell. He is wearing jeans and a blue shirt that fits him perfectly. Everything seems to fit him anyway. My parents are out for dinner.

"Hello Miss Blush," he teases me with a playful smile.

"Hi, Mister Bad Jokes," I reply with a winning smile.

"Good one," he congratulates me, nodding, and lifts his hand for a high five.

We slap hands before walking to his car. He puts on Shawn Mendes' music because he knows I love it.

"Where are we going?" I ask him while watching the landscape.

"Some friends are having a kind of party, so I would like us to go."

"I don't really like parties," I tell him.

"It's not the noisy sort. Trust me." I don't reply and just wait for us to arrive.

Someone opens the door to us, a bottle of vodka in hand. It's the guy I saw with Shawn in the cafeteria. He is wearing a long pink T-shirt. His curly blond hair looks funny and he is wearing a pair of shorts that are way too small for him. *Weird character*. His comic face only inspires affection though.

"Hey guys, Shawn is here," he shouts behind him before looking back at us. "With Princess Cinderella," he adds quietly with a funny smile. Shawn snatches the bottle from his friend's hand, and he frowns and then giggles. I move behind Shawn because I don't know what to think.

"It's not time to drink," Shawn tells him. "Fifame, this is my friend Chester. Chester this is Fifame my... girlfriend." I blush when he says that I am his girlfriend. We've only known each other since last week and here we are talking about a relationship. I didn't know before if we were a couple or not, because we are just going around kissing and then back to talking as if nothing happened.

Chester's face lights up; he throws his arm over my shoulders to guide me inside. Shawn is following us and I know he is making fun of me, of the way I am tense. Four people are sitting in the living room.

"Hey guys, it's Shawn's girlfriend," he announces like it's the greatest news in the world. They all stand up except one of them.

"I'm Kate," a brunette with blue eyes tells me and hugs me.

"Nice to meet you," I say.

"Caroline," the other girl looking exactly like Kate says. "Kate's sister," she adds.

"I think, I guessed," I say with a ridiculous smile. They are so similar. I don't know if I could tell them apart, but for tonight, I am going to concentrate on their clothes.

"Liam," one with a British accent tells me.

"Nice to meet you." My discomfort has passed and I feel more comfortable with them if we forget the blond guy sitting and staring at me strangely. We finally sit and

I don't know how it happened but I'm between the blond guy and Shawn. The boy, whose name I still don't know, is leaning against the couch and I feel his eyes burning my back. I hold Shawn's hand tightly.

"Are you okay?" Shawn asks me, frowning and I nod. It's as if no one has noticed the silent guy. The possibility that he could be a ghost that I'm the only one able to see crosses my mind, but I laugh at that ridiculous thought. But what if...? He emits a strange aura. Or maybe I shouldn't have watched so many horror movies.

"So, tell me everything. I just got back from a short internship in Ottawa and here I am with my best friend and his girlfriend," states Chester with too much excitement. He is just next to Shawn, sitting slantwise on the sofa.

"Yeah, none of us was informed of this. Were you hiding her?" Liam continues. All their eyes are on us. I wonder how it could have been if Dylan and Hailey were as interested in my life as Shawn's friends are in his.

"Since when do you know each other?" Caroline asks, a leg over her sister's.

"Last week," Shawn answers simply.

Their eyes go wide and Liam even spits his Coke out into the cup. I do understand their surprise. "And you are already dating?" Liam asks.

"I think we are," I answer shyly. I don't want them to think that I am easy. The fact is just that I really liked Shawn since the day I met him — even if it sounds cliché. I do like everything about him, even if I don't know him deeply. I don't think time should count if you feel comfortable with someone. I look at their different expressions, ready to hear all the judgements.

53

"That's cool if you guys like it like that," Kate finally says after a long silence. They all nod and shrug. Wow! That is incredible. "Let's start," Kate says and stands up.

"Tonight, it's karaoke," Chester gushes while clapping his hands like a girl. I don't know why but I really like him.

"You start."

I look around and then back at Kate, who is pointing me. "Me?" My heart starts beating faster.

"Sure," she says.

"Why me?" I don't know why they want me to start. "I have an ugly voice," I tell them.

"Everyone here has an ugly voice," she asserts and they all nod. I sigh and stand up. They put on "Hello" by Adele and I start to sing slowly. Having my eyes on Shawn's helps me to keep going. I admire the curves of his lips. They keep all my focus. Even though I am singing wrong, it's like I am singing well for him. I forget about the weird guy and sing "Roar" by Katy Perry with joy. I feel comfortable here.

"I confirm that your voice is deeply ugly but nice," Chester teases me and I roll my eyes but smile.

"Let's hear yours," I challenge him, sticking out my tongue like a child.

"Give me that microphone," he says and stands up. He sings "Happy" by Pharrell William with weird moves. Everyone is laughing except Mister Spectator. Chester beckons me and I stand up. We try to dance and everyone laughs harder.

"Jesus, you guys dance worse than you sing," Liam laughs.

On his turn, Shawn has to sing "When You're Ready" by Shawn Mendes. I had forgotten that he has this awesome voice. Everyone is staring at him, absorbed by his voice. The notes that come out of his mouth fill my ears like paradise. His eyes are glued to mine. When he is done, my mouth is still open.

"Close your mouth, you'll catch a fly," he teases me after sitting back down.

"You guys are big liars," I tell them with a small pout.

"Not liars, truth savers. Besides, Shawn sings when he drives so you couldn't have not known he sings well," Caroline corrects me. Most of the twins I have met in my life are physically alike but still very different. But Caroline and Kate are absolutely alike. They look at me the same way, drink the same way, laugh almost the same way. They just have different voices. It might send me mad if I was with them all the same.

We all talk for hours. I learn more about their group. They have known one another since secondary school except Shawn and Chester who met at elementary school. Chester and Shawn's first encounter is one of the weirdest I have heard of in my entire life. In elementary school, Chester was being bullied because he laughed at everything and some children found it annoying. One day, they decided to scare him and beat him up, but at the same time he stole Shawn's calculator (I'm not sure why he had one — we weren't allowed one until eighth or ninth grade) because he loved numbers and Shawn didn't want to give it to him. Chester asked him even though they had never even talked to each other before. So, Shawn noticed it and came back to school because he knew Chester was still inside. He tried to stop the boys hurting him but they were much stronger. Shawn and Chester, who were much smarter, started saying things to confuse them. Finally, the three boys ended up crying and avoiding Shawn and Chester for the rest of elementary school. I don't know what they said to them. Shawn and Chester just said, "We said things to them." Then, Shawn gave his calculator to Chester as friendship gift and Chester gave him a language book for children. And they became best friends.

***

Still no one is talking to the silent guy and he doesn't talk to anyone either. An urgent desire to go to the bathroom takes me.

"Can I use your bathroom?" I ask everyone since I don't know whose home it is.

"Sure, you can. Just the last door in the corridor," Chester answers.

I thank him and stand up. On my way, I look around. The home looks like Chester. They are so many colors that it's dazzling. There is strange art on the walls. One is a kind of lion-bird wearing Egyptian clothes and dark glasses. I can't help but chuckle at the cool look of the animal in the picture. He is class. Once I am done, I look at myself in the mirror, I do look happy. I can't thank Shawn enough for this.

I finally walk out of the toilets, looking at my feet and trying to walk on an imaginary tightrope on the floor. I bump into someone, gasp and back away. It is the weird guy. He has an odd smile on his face. I am backing away as he is walking to me. My heart is pounding in my chest and I just want to disappear. The corridor is quite long.

"H-Hi. You like mangoes?" I start to stay nervously. The fear is taking over my mind. "Or do you like flowers?" I have a nervous smile on my face. The light is sparkling like in the horror movies and an irrepressible desire to vomit takes me. He raises his hand and tries to touch me. The light goes off and I hear many doors open and shouting and there are hands touching me. I shout and try to run away but the light is turned back on.

I don't look around and just run but a hand grabs my wrist and turns me towards him… Shawn? I look around and everyone is looking at me and laughing. "What? What is so funny?" I ask them, lost.

"It was a joke." Shawn explains to me. I give him a confused look and look round at each of them. My eyes land on the guy. "This is Tom. He is mute and he likes playing that kind of game. As you were coming, we thought it would be a good idea."

On one hand, I feel sorry for Tom, it can't be easy not being able to speak. But on the other hand, I am furious with all of them. I could have died of fear.

"And you think this is funny?" I bawl. They are all looking at me now apologetically, but I am not taking it. I don't know why, but through them I am seeing all the other people who once made fun of me, they are reminding me of such bad memories.

"Don't cry please. We are sorry," Liam tries to make it up with me.

I was really afraid and the strong emotions I'm feeling are now making me cry. I wipe the tears away with the back of my hand and walk to the door. "Wait, we are sorry," Shawn is begging, walking behind me, but I don't listen to him. He grabs my wrist and I snatch it away.

"Just leave me alone," I tell him and open the door.

I am really pissed off. For all they knew I could have had a heart condition, yet they just decided to play such a stupid game. I walk out, Shawn behind me.

"Please, at least let me drive you back home," he continues. I remember that I don't have my car with me. He opens his and we get in silently.

"Please Fifa, I'm sorry," he tells me but I just concentrate on the landscape. "Can a kangaroo jump higher than a house?" Then: "Of course, a house doesn't jump at all."

If he thinks that a joke will make me forget the bad taste of another one, he is deluding himself. During the trip he tries several times to make me laugh but for once, it is really annoying instead of pleasing me. As soon as he parks on my driveway, I walk inside without even looking at him. When I enter, my parents are sitting on the couch, laughing and talking.

"Hey princess, how was your evening?" my mother asks me.

"It sucked," I answer before thinking. I have never said these kinds of words to my parents, so it is very weird. I walk straight to my room without having dinner. I don't answer Shawn's texts and just go to sleep. The whole scene of the evening is playing again and again in my mind. I can't believe they are so like them, like those people from my past.

CHAPTER TEN

S unday, I wake up in a bad mood. However, I glance at my phone to check if he's texted me, but he hasn't and I am somehow disappointed. But I am mostly afraid that all my doubts were justified. I have always been afraid that Shawn is too perfect to be real, too afraid that he may be playing a game. And secretly, I am scared that he is not really who he seems to be. My heart sinks as these thoughts travel through my mind. He seems so sincere that I can't even think about such a terrible possibility, but my head is reminding me that it is possible. It's reminding me that all the people who entered my life and looked kind always took any opportunity to make fun of me... Maybe Shawn is like them. Maybe he is now done with his wicked game.

I stare at his photos for ages before watching a very old episode of "Tom and Jerry" on my phone. But even one of the funniest cartoons is not making me laugh or even smile. Shawn is now the only one able to that. Hours later, I finally leave my bed, brush my teeth and walk slowly to the kitchen. I'm wearing "Tom and Jerry" pants and sweater which are far too big for me. My slippers are cats" faces. My hair is incredibly ugly but I don't care.

I don't look at anyone when I walk into the kitchen, I mechanically grab the box of cereal and a bowl. I pour it into the bowl and add milk. I sit down and eat, deep in my thoughts, wondering if I should call Shawn or not.

"Fifa, are you okay?" I lift my head up to my father who once again has the same magazine in his hands. What is he even reading every day? He observes me, curious.

"I'm..." I start but voices cut me off.

"I'm so glad you helped me with all those books. My husband doesn't read them any more, and I needed space for mine," I hear my mother's voice say.

"It's a pleasure; I will read them to my grandma. She likes art." That voice... it's his. As they enter the kitchen, the spoon is only inches from my open mouth. My eyes land on him; he's wearing a short and a grey sweater making him so... sexy. And the best time he found to show up is when I look like a yeti. I put the spoon back in the bowl. All right, it fell in the bowl.

"Hey sweetie. Look who is here. He came for you, but I didn't know if you were awake. I suggested he help me to clean up the library."

I know she is lying; it's about one o'clock and she knows I don't sleep that much. I am sure she took the opportunity to ask him weird questions. If mother were not a doctor, she would have been a policewoman or an inspector or a journalist. She is overly nosy. Shawn has a huge smile on the face. I don't know what it is that's bothering me, but I can't help but think that it's a fake smile. I get up blankly and walk to my room. When I reach the stairs, my mother asks, "Where are you going?"

"My room." I continue to walk. I know it's childish, but I just want to avoid Shawn. I don't want to become so obsessed with him that when everything falls apart, it'll be right in my face. I don't want to fall in love with someone who may be lying or using me. I know this is stupid. Although I don't know that Shawn has done anything that bad, I can't brush my bad thoughts away.

Once I'm back in my room, someone knocks at my door. I sigh. "Come in." Shawn appears with a nervous look. I don't think I have ever seen him nervous before.

"What are you doing in my house?" I ask curtly.

"I... I just wanted to see you."

"Well... now that you have seen me, you can go," I say, calmer now.

"Listen, I'm sorry for yesterday. Please just don't do that," he begs me.

I try to not look at him and focus on the wall. I just don't want to believe in us, to end up crying and even more depressed than before. I am afraid that if I look at him, into his eyes, I will lose my resolve. I am a coward, but I prefer that to suffering. He walks to me, but I look away. He grabs my wrist. I don't even have the strength to remove it, because I want his skin against mine. He pulls me closer to him and I try to get away but my body doesn't agree. He forces me to look at him by turning my face to his, but I still look away.

"Are you sure this is still about that joke or are you just taking it as an opportunity to break up with me?" As the words leave his mouth, it pains me deeply. I don't want to suffer later and even less now. I haven't even gotten through the pain of years ago.

"Just leave," I beg him, my voice shaking. I know that if this continues, I may jump on him and kiss him till tonight. I may forget that I don't want to suffer.

"I'm not leaving. I promised that I won't. Remember?" He puts his hands on my neck and our foreheads touch. His desperate breathing mingles with mine as my heartbeat accelerates. "Tell me what I can do to make you forgive me," he asks me through a breath. My whole body is shaking. He seems to not mind my appearance.

My lips are just asking to join his, but I am struggling. He, however, joins his lips to mine and I give in.

A crazy feeling of well-being unfolds in me, while his tongue dances with mine. His lips are so good against mine. I'm savoring... I am savoring it, but the images remain in my memory. Their stupid joke yesterday, what happened a few years ago. I detach myself from him and grit my teeth not to cry. I turn my back on him and cross my arms.

"Please, leave," I try to articulate. He waits a few seconds, probably lost and confused by my behavior, but finally leaves. I take a deep breath, head to the bathroom to take a long shower and braid my hair.

Once done, I sit for a long time, staring at Shawn's pictures on my phone, trying to remember the effect of his lips on mine. Each time that I want to call him and just tell him to come back, I remember, always remember. I keep remembering why I was depressed for so many years.

"Sweetie?" I hear Mom call me from the open door. I am lying in bed, face buried in my pillow. I groan. "Come and have lunch, please."

I know what she thinks. She thinks that I am going back to my depressed state, that I will stop eating again, that Shawn broke my heart, but I am the one who did it. I am not hungry. I just want Shawn, but my stupidity is pushing me to avoid him. I stand up, then sit and put on my shoes without looking at her. I stand up again slowly. "Let's go," I tell her through a sigh.

She looks sad and I don't want her to. During lunch, I am struggling to eat. I have fought with myself over the years to not make them feel what I feel inside, but I am failing. "Did Shawn do anything wrong?" my father asks me. His tone is not at all threatening but sympathetic. *Shawn played a bad joke on me with his friends.* I don't think that is valid reason to avoid him. The truth is that I have not and will never get through my depression.

"No Dad," I answer simply.

"What's wrong then? He came downstairs looking so hurt," my mother tells me.

Thanks for reminding me I am the bad person, acting like this. I stand up. "Nothing," I answer before putting my plate in the sink.

I head to my room and work for the whole day. I stare at my phone most of the time, waiting for a message from Shawn but get no text. What was I even expecting? I broke the only heart that knew mine.

CHAPTER ELEVEN

*H*appiness tip two: Never keep any bad feeling inside your heart. Let it go. I miss you.

I miss you too. I read the text from Shawn several times, making me feel worse. I like this boy so much that I can't handle it. I groan and get up. I do everything dejectedly. I know that I have let depression back in, but I just don't want to fight with *her*. Depression doesn't need a big deal to show up. It's so simple to let the sadness take over your life. I wear a purple dress and put my hair in a bun, as usual. I put on my sneakers, take my bag and go downstairs. Fortunately, my parents are already gone to work since my mother's break is over. I grab an apple and take my way to U.T. This will be another long day.

I enter the class later than usual, because I had to gather all my strength to prepare myself to see Shawn. Once I step in, I spot him sitting at his usual place, just next to mine. My body is shaking; I might never be ready to see him again. I sit near a guy at the other side of the class because it is the only free place quite close to the front and far from Shawn. Our eyes meet and I shiver; I want to look away, but I can't. He looks hurt. He is the first one to look away. During the class, the boy next to me doesn't take any notice of me. At least with Shawn, we discuss the class and try to understand it together.

At the end of the class, I am among the first ones to leave. This is the first time though. Outside, I see him walking towards me and I quickly look for an escape. I locate Hailey and Dylan and even though I don't want to be friends with them any more, I don't want to talk to Shawn. *You do want to. Just shut up.* They are both laughing when I reach them. I just laugh along with them. Shawn stops in the middle of the hallway, looking at me with a lost expression. He finally walks away. As soon as he leaves, I head to my second class without eating. The rest of the day, and even the week is so empty. I avoid him the first two days but after that, he doesn't try to talk to me any more.

Happiness tip three: Believe that you deserve the best.

I don't believe at all that I deserve anything good. I don't deserve Shawn. It has been a week already that Shawn and I are on bad terms. I miss him so badly. I am done with my classes today. I am walking out of the faculty when someone grabs me and throws me over his shoulder like a sack of potatoes. It just takes me some seconds to notice that it's Chester.

"What are you doing? Let go of me!" I protest. People are looking at us briefly, but they'd rather mind their own business. I hit Chester's back and struggle. "Chester, I am serious!"

"Chocolate princess just calm down," he teases me. He is much stronger than he looks. I finally surrender and cross my arms and pout. He walks out of the faculty to reach an isolated area of the university.

"Are you going to kill me?" I ask him, only half joking.

He walks behind a building and puts me down. I know perfectly why we are here. There is only one reason. When I turn around and see Shawn, leaning against a wall and looking at the sky, my doubts are confirmed. He looks so perfect, perfectly wrong for me. My heart beats quickly in my chest but I don't want to run away.

"I don't like seeing my best friend like this and I know we fucked up, but please forgive us," says Chester seriously.

Shawn turns his gaze on us. Surprise is clear on his face. Chester waves at him and quickly walks away after winking at me. I take a deep breath, filling my lungs with as much air as possible. I clumsily walk to Shawn, my heart beating wildly. He is immobile, staring at me. I want to run away. Paradoxically, I want to talk to him, to apologize, to stick the pieces back together. I finally stop in front of him, twisting my fingers.

"He told me to meet him here. I knew it was to do something stupid," Shawn tries to joke but I know he is nervous. We stay silent for a while before I decide to break the silence.

"I'm sorry."

He looks at me, taken aback. "Sorry?"

"Yes, I acted like a dummy instead of talking to you about what is really annoying me. I'm thankful to Chester for bringing me here," I tell him, avoiding eyes contact.

"And what is annoying you?" he asks too gently, making me feel worse. After my reaction to what happened, here he is caring that much about me.

"Not annoying, scaring I meant," I start. I don't really know where to start, what to say. "I'm just afraid," I whisper hastily.

"Of what? Of... me?" he asks, making me face him, his fingers under my chin.

"No... I don't know...I—," I start to panic.

Shawn places his hands on my cheeks, squeezing them with his thumbs. His breath hits my skin. "Tell me," he whispers.

"I don't want to suffer, Shawn. I know that I haven't yet recovered from my depression and I'm afraid that it will hurt you or that everything will blow up in my face," I tell him. A sob tears my throat and I struggle to not cry.

"Depression?" I don't know if I am ready to talk about all this to him. All what happened before and why I am so sad. I don't know how to answer to the first serious question he has ever asked me.

"When you played your stupid joke, I thought you guys were going to be like all those people who make fun of me." I choose to be honest but to ignore the mention of the depression. "I thought you were making fun of me and my feelings too," I add lower.

"It was just a stupid joke as you said and I'm deeply sorry, Fifa. Tom just wanted to transform his sad state into something funny and that's why we support him." I really do understand what he's saying. It can't be easy for Tom to be mute. He just wanted a way to have some fun and it fell on me. "And what depression, tell me? Is that the point? Are you depressed or have you been? Have you talked to anyone about it? Have you seen any specialists?" he persists.

My eyes are buried in his, so I can't even try to lie to him. I don't know how to tell him all that has happened, I don't know if I will be able to say it. "I don't want to talk about it now," I answer honestly. He squeezes my cheeks softly.

"All right. But you know that you have to talk to someone about it, don't you?" he replies, and I nod. "I know some people think that they can overcome it alone but that's also a part of depression. It pushes you to find a reason to stay alone. I'm here for you. Please know that. You're very important to me."

I like to hear him talk to me that way, with confidence. I like to hear him promise me so many things. I like believing that it may become true one day. I rest my head against his chest that is moving slowly. It is quite cold and dark clouds are showing up in the sky. I hear his heartbeat against my ear; I love the music of it. I think this is going to be my favorite melody. He wraps his arms around my waist and pulls me closer to him before resting his chin on my head. I hug him back. "I missed you," I whisper.

"I did also. I was going crazy," he replies and I smile.

After some minutes he finally separates from me. I lift my head up to catch his lips. I've been dreaming of his lips against mine throughout the last week. His moist and devilishly soft lips massage mine. My hands are drowning in his brown hair while he is hugging me harder. As it starts to rain, we pull apart. We smile to each other. He puts his arm around my shoulders, I put mine on his back, leaning against him, and we walk to the car. I am so glad to have him back. My stomach gurgles as soon as we get in the car and we burst out laughing. I think that my stomach was waiting for us to get back together before showing its suffering. The droplets of water fall on the windows while it rains harder. The coldness makes me shiver. I look at Shawn, I admire him. Without a doubt, I am falling in love with him.

***

"When was the last time you ate?" Shawn asks me when we are a few blocks away from my house.

"This morning," I answer him while skipping through the stations on the radio.

"And that was?"

"Are you a nutritionist now?" I tease him, looking over at him.

"Don't avoid my question. I see you coming."

I chuckle. "An apple," I tell him without mentioning that I barely ate yesterday.

"I should give you a spanking, you know?" he threatens, and I laugh.

"Go on," I provoke him. I put on some Latino music that I don't know. The music is slow and melodious.

He parks the car; we're in mine because he didn't bring his to college. We quickly walk into the house because of the rain. As I had quit most of the clubs, it's earlier than usual. It is about five. To my surprise, my parents are here. My dad is working in a corner of the big living room while my mother is getting ready for her shift. They look at us, surprised.

"Hello, I'm just passing through, we are going back out," I tell them.

"All right," mother answers.

I head to my room and get ready as quickly as I can before they kill Shawn with all their questions. Before leaving the living room though, I hear a few parts of their conversation.

"Did your grandmother like the books?" my mother asks Shawn.

"She did. I now have to read her one every night," Shawn answers

"See, Ronel, your books are now useful." My mother is always in such a teasing mood.

I return to the living room, grab Shawn's hand and walk quickly outside with an umbrella. I had heard what my mother had said: "So aren't you planning to live together?"

"Did I imagine it or did my mother ask you if we are planning to live together?" I say, quite embarrassed by her behavior. I have just started dating Shawn and she has chosen to embarrass him as much as she can. I would like to see him more often, to wake up with him but it's too early. By flying too fast, I could crash quickly.

"She did," he answers laughing. I chuckle too. "My mother was also like that, you know? I mean clumsy and funny," he tells me nostalgically. I smile to him and squeeze his thigh.

"I'm sure she was lovely." I sing along with Shawn Mendes' songs on the way. We finally stop in front of Alicio and Alessia's restaurant. I am obviously glad to come back here. The restaurant is called the "Double A". It is a quite weird name for an Italian restaurant but never mind. Shawn parks the car on the sidewalk in front of the restaurant.

"Thank God we are finally here, I would have died from your ugly voice," he complains, and I roll my eyes. I want to get out, but the doors are locked. "Kiss me first," he says in a bossy tone. I smile and roll my eyes but softly press my lips against his; he smiles against my lips. It is delightful to have him back. If Chester hadn't done what he did, I could have lost a good thing. I know that I still have so much to deal with, so many black thoughts and demons inside me but I want Shawn to help me. The rain has stopped but it is still cold, thankfully I had put on a jacket. As soon as we enter the Double A, my eyes land on Chester, guzzling a huge pile of spaghetti. Tom is also there. They are having a kind of eating competition. Chester has several empty bowls at his side and some people are standing around and cheering.

71

"Here he is practicing his favorite sport: eating." I chuckle at Shawn's remark and we walk over to them.

Chester has just finished his food and claps his hands vigorously. "And you're the Italian here?" he teases Tom who can't even hear what he's saying. He's just sitting on a chair, exhausted. This is funny. They turn to us. "They are finally done kissing," he teases us, saying it too loudly, making me blush. Tom's eyes and mine meet; he looks worried about my reaction, but I smile to him and he smiles back, relieved. We all sit at a table.

"Sweetie, *gratias*. You're back. You are so beautiful," Alessia tells me and kisses me on the cheeks. I like this atmosphere. I could have never gotten the chance for this if I were shut in my room. She walks to the kitchen after pinching my cheeks.

"Tom is mute but he can hear. His vocal cords were paralyzed when he was younger. He was singer," Shawn tells me and I feel sorrier for Tom.

"Why did you say he's Italian?" I ask Chester.

"He is Alessia and Alicio's son. But I'm more Italian than him. At least as far as food is concerned," Chester says and we laugh, even Tom.

"Tom is a quite strange name for an Italian," I say.

"His —" Tom raises his hand for Chester to stop talking. He opens his bag and takes a book note and a pen. He writes something down and gives it to me.

"My parents like traveling, so they gave us names from different cultures. My brothers are living in other countries too," I read.

"That's nice," I tell him through a smile. "But you know, I know sign language," I sign to him and everyone looks surprised.

"I'm glad to know it," Tom tells me through signs.

We finally eat and chat, laughing more than anyone else here. Shawn and Chester are telling their whole stock of jokes. My stomach pains me more by laughing than eating too much of this tasty food.

"Here you have another apple juice," Alessia says and puts the bottle on the table.

"Thank you," I smile to her.

Since I'm the only customer fond of apple juice, they added it to the menu. Chester tries to take the bottle but I slap his hand.

"Don't touch my apple juice," I warn him, like a spoiled child, I admit.

"Yeah Chester, don't touch my girl's apple juice," Shawn adds but takes the bottle to drink a long sip.

My mouth falls open, while the three boys look amused.

"I'm breaking up with you," I say and pout.

Shawn has a big smirk on the face. He pulls me closer to him. I thought he was going to kiss me but he starts to tickle me and I laugh too loudly.

"So?" he says.

"I'm not breaking up," I say, still shaken with laughter and he releases me.

"Cool," Shawn and Chester say together while Chester drinks the rest of the drink.

Alessia is already coming back with another one.

"On the house," she says to me. "You guys pay for the other two," she says to Shawn and Chester and I laugh. I stick my tongue out to them before drinking my juice.

***

"See you guys," I tell them while putting on my jacket. Shawn puts his hand on my back. Chester pulls me to him and hugs me, then kisses me on both cheeks like Alicio and Alessia do.

"Chester, if you want to steal my girlfriend, just tell me," Shawn jokes but I feel a mildly threatening tone behind it.

"It's coming," Chester replies and sticks his tongue out at him. Shawn rolls his eyes but smiles. Tom hugs me too.

"See you guys at your wedding," Chester shouts as we are leaving and I can't help but giggle, embarrassed. This boy is so weird and funny and clumsy. I drive to Shawn's and park in front of the house.

"Say hello to Frida," I tell him.

"Okay."

I choose to play his game and lock the doors. He turns to me playfully. "Open," he orders.

"Kiss me first," I reply.

"No," he protests and my smile drops. "So open." I don't know if he is joking or not because he has a serious look. What if he is done with me now? My mouth falls open and I unlock the door. He walks out without a word. I am staring straight in front of me, trying to understand what just happened. Taps on my window bring me back to reality. Shawn's face appears behind it with a playful grin. He opens the door and speaks, "Come." He is holding himself from laughing.

Once I am out of the car, he closes the door. "How can you think that I would miss an opportunity..." He pushes me softly against the car and puts his hands to my sides. Then he says, "To kiss those lips."

I am taken aback at first, but I finally cross my arms over my chest and pout, looking away and trying to not kiss him. He is too close to me. "You should stop your stupid jokes," I warn him and mean it.

"Come on, your face was so funny. I don't get why you think that I can make fun of you this way." I am still looking away, trying to look angry but it is quite difficult. "Come on baby," he begs through his playful smile. The word baby kills me. He just called me *baby*. I blink rapidly, trying not to smile. The rain is starting again but stays light. "Kiss me." The way he says it makes me shiver, his voice is so deep and sensual. He presses his lips against my neck and slowly moves back up to my lips. The droplets of water falling on our skin, plus the kiss make me lose my mind. I kiss him back, feverishly. I put my arms around his neck and pull him closer to me. I don't control the moan that leaves my mouth and makes him smile against me. After some minutes and because of the rain getting heavier, we kiss one last time. He strokes my cheeks with his thumbs and kisses my forehead.

"You're perfect," he sighs.

"Perfectly wrong for such a flawless boy like you?" I add and he smiles.

"No, just perfect." I smile at him and he kisses me one last time before pulling away from me.

"Take care and text me as soon as you get home," he says, and I nod.

I choose to not keep any bad feelings inside me any more. I choose to let go any bad feelings and to keep all the good ones. I choose all the nice and amazing feelings that Shawn makes me feel.

CHAPTER TWELVE

S hawn and I are done with our classes for the day. It's already Thursday and I am so impatient for the weekend. I do love working but I prefer the weekend to the rest of the week.

"Chester showed them his buttocks just to assure them that he doesn't have any spots on it. Geez. Where did I find a fiend like that?" Shawn grumbles as he rolls his eyes; I can't help but laugh.

We are walking, on our way to the parking lot. Shawn drove me to school this morning.

"I knew you guys loved me, you're always talking about me." Chester has just appeared from nowhere. He puts an arm around each of our shoulders, and we keep walking.

He kisses me on the cheek and turns to Shawn, but Shawn threatens, "Do that and I will kill you."

"If I don't have the right to show my love to my best friend..." he mumbles, and I chuckle.

"You guys are fighting most of the time, but you are still the best friends I've never met," I laugh. I have been with the two of them throughout the week and they are as close as brothers.

"Hello guys... Fifa." I look and see Caroline who has just spoken. I was so concentrated on the two boys that I didn't notice when Caroline, Kate and Tom joined us. We stop and the three of them are avoiding eye contact with me.

"It's fine, guys." I tell them and their faces light up. "This weekend, my parents are in Ottawa, I would like you to come over for a barbecue in my garden," I suggest.

"I love you, Fifa," Chester says while rubbing his stomach and everyone laughs.

"Stop talking to my girl, Ches." Chester kisses the air, while looking at Shawn. "Hold me back or I will kill him," Shawn threatens and Chester rolls his eyes and winks.

***

With Shawn and Chester's help, we are done setting everything up for the barbecue. I couldn't do my laundry last night, so I did it this morning after jogging. I seasoned pieces of beef and chicken with the best spices ever and then dipped them in a spicy tomato sauce. I also made salad and potatoes. I concocted a special drink from Benin called bissap and of course, bought some apple juice. The others arrive and I open the door to them with a warm smile.

"Welcome," I tell them.

"Thanks for inviting us," Liam grins.

I am grilling the meat with Shawn while they are sitting and talking.

"You're so beautiful when you cook," Shawn whispers. My stomach flutters because of his sensual voice.

"I agree," Chester says behind me.

He stretches his arm to grab some meat from the plate. I slap his hand; he shakes it and pouts.

"Don't touch," I scold.

"Now you're ugly," he mumbles and sticks his tongue out at me.

"Thank you," I reply and do the same.

We finally sit together around the table to eat.

"Sorry again for the last time," Kate says. I give her a small smile.

"Never mind but no more stupid jokes okay?" I state to all of them.

They all nod except Chester.

"Just one from time to time," he says with a wicked look, making me roll my eyes but also smile.

During the lunch, Chester pours the sauce on me, the whole bowl on my white dress.

"Oops," he says with a wicked voice.

Everyone is staring at me, narrowed eyes and worried. They are afraid that I may take it bad. However, I don't know why, but I laugh at the silliness of Chester. He is pissed off because of the meat I didn't give to him. I wipe the sauce off my dress and spread it on his shirt. I burst out laughing; I laugh so hard that they are all looking at me with raised eyebrows. Chester stands up and pulls my chair; I fall on the floor. He is also laughing. I want to kill him, but I can't even stand up because I am laughing too much. Everyone finally joins in and we spend more time laughing and joking than actually eating.

"Thank you so much for a great time, Fifa," Liam says as I hug him goodbye.

"You guys are welcome, and I really enjoyed spending time with you."

They finally leave, leaving just Shawn and me in the house. We cleaned up together before they left, except Chester who said that today is the international day of *someone in a group doesn't clean*. We all laughed at his bad reason but decided to not argue because Chester is a big baby and he really acts like he is.

***

I go to my room and Shawn turns to me. He is sitting by my window, staring at the stars, the same way I love to. The sky is such a wonderful thing, especially at night. I love to gaze at the stars, believing that anything is possible and everything will be fine. I love the way the stars are bright, despite the darkness. It makes me believe that depression is not my friend, that I don't deserve it. No one deserves that fire in the heart, and that constant sadness. I put my wet hair in a bun because I just bathed, I will braid it before sleeping. I make my way over to Shawn. Apart from the stars, this man gives me hope. With him, I feel happy, or at least much better. I sit between his legs, my back against his chest and my head just below his chin. We silently stare at the stars; we quietly enjoy each other.

"I just want you to be happy," whispers Shawn so softly that I could hardly hear him.

"What?" I ask. He blenches as if I woke him up from a dream.

I lift my head up to look at him. There is something in his gaze that is different, different from Shawn's gaze. It is like a dark field covering a joyful and heavenly one. An ocean of sadness is filling his eyes, and he is fighting against it. But I am too aware of what it is, to think that he is fine.

"Nothing, sorry," he stammers. I frown, he is still looking at the sky, avoiding eye contact with me. I gently put my hand on his cheek and stroke it.

"You can talk to me, you know," I tell him softly. He looks at me, his eyes are shining.

"Nothing is wrong. I was just thinking," he softly replies, putting his arms around me; he pulls me closer to him. He holds me so tightly. Shawn seems afraid of me leaving, of me falling. "Promise me that you will try to avoid it," he says quietly, looking into my eyes. I don't know if he is still talking to me. It is as if there is a third person here, whom Shawn is talking to.

"Avoid what?"

"Sadness, depression. Promise it."

I pull my back from his chest and turn to face him. I try to see through him, to understand him but there is a huge barrier in the way. "I promise," I quietly answer even though it is impossible. Sadness is impossible to avoid, maybe we should just face it and continue on our way instead of running away from it.

I wrap my arms around his shoulders and kneel down to hug him. He tightens his hold on me, his scent fills my nostrils. "You are wonderful," he whispers against my neck.

"So are you." I kiss him gently, he runs his hands through my hair, his tongue meets mine and our souls connect. I can't handle this wonderful well-being that takes over me each time that Shawn is around. The way he bites my bottom lip and holds my waist drives me crazy. I am still on my knees. I try to stand without letting go of him, but I lose my balance. I drag him as I fall and we both find ourselves on the floor. He is on top of me but is supporting his weight with his elbows. He moves to lie next to me and we burst out laughing.

"At least, we always fall together, as a couple," he jokes and I roll onto my side to look at him.

"And I wish it to always be like that," I whisper, eyes buried in his.

"It will," he assures me with a smile. Then, he pulls me in for another long kiss. A soft and sweet kiss, the way I love it.

CHAPTER THIRTEEN

*H*appiness tip seven: Choose the right people to surround you. This text has the usual effect of Shawn's texts on me. As with anything that comes from Shawn, it pleases me. It's been about two months since I met Shawn. The last two months have been my best September and October ever. I read once again last week's tip: laughter is the best medicine. That tip is actually true. With Shawn and Chester, any opportunity to have fun is a precious gift. I have never laughed this much in my life and the last week has been the craziest. Since they know that Dylan and Hailey hate yellow, they came to school dressed completely in yellow. They even wore yellow glasses and wrote on their shirts "Yellow is not for the people below."

The worst thing is that they showed up at the college and followed Dylan and Hailey almost everywhere. This was so funny but silly. When I asked Shawn why he was acting like that, because for someone who likes happiness, he was making some other people really angry, he simply replied "To be happy, you also have to not love everyone." Then, I asked him to explain what he meant and he did. We were in the middle of the hallway, everyone was staring at us and Shawn was giving them bright smiles. "If you really want to be happy, you don't have to force yourself to love people. You can choose who you want to hang out with. Remember tip five: No one is meant to love everyone." And for the end of the spectacle, they waited for Dylan and Hailey to leave the school.

Why? Because they rented a yellow car for the day. So, when my old fake friends arrived in the parking lot, they looked embarrassed and disgusted. I stayed in my car to watch them. Shawn was driving and Chester whistled at Dylan and Hailey before they left. Shawn winked at me and I rolled my eyes with a smile.

Lying down on my bed, I realize how true tip seven is. I never really felt good when I was hanging out with Dylan and Hailey. During the last weeks with Shawn's friends, everything seems better. With them, I am myself: we laugh, joke, have fun together. No one is ashamed of anyone. With these wonderful six people, I feel good. Although Tom is not at our college, he hangs out with us sometimes and I admire how positive he is about his situation. Then, I notice how lucky I am to not have any kind of physical disability, how much I should thank God for all these gifts. Because Tom, even though he can't speak, is happy because he can walk, hear, and simply live. We are sometimes so focused on our problems that we forget our blessings. This is what he has taught me, and Shawn had turned it into happiness tip four: Be thankful for what you have.

I finally decide to get up, I am wearing Kaeloo pajamas. *Team cartoons till death.* I quickly shower and head back to my room. Once inside, I start the thing I hate doing the most: choosing what to wear. This is such a stressful thing because even if you have thousands of clothes, you still feel like you don't have anything to wear. This is the most stressful moment every day except when I just throw anything on. But now it is different, I can't just wear any random thing. *Because of Shawn,* my consciousness tells me with a smirk but I ignore it. But it is true, I should always look good for him. I should avoid looking like a yeti like the day he came around after our fight. I was a physical disaster. I try on some clothes and even when they look nice in the wardrobe, once on me, they are ugly, or I am ugly.

I try on and try on clothes. Sometimes I put on something that I tried just a few minutes ago to check out if it will fit me now, but it doesn't. I glance at the clock and I am almost late for school. Panic takes over me and I breath slowly to handle my stress. I finally decide to wear jeans and a white long-sleeved top. *All this time for that?* my consciousness whines in annoyance. As if I were not late enough, my eyes stop on my reflection in the mirror and I stop too. I am still in my underwear. Sometimes I really like my body and all my curves, but sometimes I hate it.

I glance at the fat on my thighs. I hopelessly lift my breasts and wish they were firmer. I stand on tiptoe and wish to be taller. I finally sigh deeply and sit on the floor. My heart which was happy earlier is now sad. My anxiety is like a fire which just needs a little bit of fuel to flare up. I lie down on the floor, staring at the ceiling, as I used to during my depressed years. *Be careful*, my consciousness warns me. Voices in my head are warning me; they are begging me to not let myself go back to depression. But when someone knows you too well, it's impossible to just make they forget you from one day to the next.

Even though Shawn is my sun, at night the moon (depression) takes what belongs to her. I belong to *her*. Tears are falling on my cheeks; memories are flying through my mind. I am trying to avoid them, but it's difficult. Depression knows every single piece of my soul, of my body; she knows how to handle me, how to possess me. I am too weak, too weak to fight against her. A sob rips my throat and several more follow. "Why am

I crying?" I cry louder and pray that my mother doesn't hear me. Any way she must be on call. "Why is it so difficult?" I grouse to myself. "Why can't you just enjoy life and stop being so depressed, Fifa?" And again, "Why are you so weak?" Finally, "Fifa... stop."

***

When I finally arrive at the college, my first class is already finished so I head to the second one. I used some makeup to hide that I cried but my eyes are still a bit red. I walk slowly across the hallways, like a zombie. Dylan and Hailey are a few meters from me. Dylan waves to me to come over. I stop in the middle of the hallway. Why do they still want to hang out with me? I don't know what to do. Walk to them and start a pathetic life again or just continue on my way?

"Hey Fifa!" Chester is calling me from the other side of the hallway. He is so loud that everyone looks at him. Shawn is standing next to him. I glance at Hailey and Dylan who are looking at me with threatening eyes and I sigh. Shawn seems worried that I might join my ex-friends. That is who they are: my ex-friends. They were never really my friends any way. They don't even deserve that name nor my attention. I have the right to choose; my life is my own. I smile shyly to Shawn and walk to them.

"Hi," I say quietly once at their side. I feel the burning eyes of the two, nasty people behind me. Shawn frowns and even Chester looks a little worried but they make no comment. Shawn says nothing about the fact that I missed a class either. My eyes and my head are hurting because of the crying, but I don't really care right now. I know that she's got a hold over me. To my big surprise, they both hug me together. I'm a little thing between them and this is so comfortable. I hold myself back from crying in public, in front of all those people. After the long hug, Shawn kisses me on the forehead. I thought Chester would also have kissed me but he doesn't. If the situation were different, I would burst out laughing.

"I don't want to die by his hands," he explains and a smile finds its way to my lips. "Goodbye, possessive boyfriend," he tells Shawn. "Goodbye, princess," he tells me and leaves. He is studying finance and is actually very smart and good with numbers.

"Do you want to leave?" Shawn asks me.

"I just arrived, I can't."

"But you're not feeling well! Your whole body has been trembling since you arrived. Geez." I hadn't even noticed. I don't know what's happening to me and I don't like the sympathetic look that Shawn is giving me.

"Please, it's just one class," I argue and he sighs. Throughout the class, he squeezes my hand and strokes the back of it with his thumb. I try to follow the lecturer, but it's quite difficult with all the thoughts that are burning my brain. I'm wondering why it keeps coming back to me, why I can't just be… happy.

We walk to the parking lot; Shawn's arm is around my shoulder as I lean against him. One earphone is in my right ear and the other one is in his left ear. "In My Blood" by Shawn Mendes is filling our ears. This song is the summary of my life. I just want someone to help me and Shawn is that someone. I always want to give up. The walls are already caving in every time that I try to take a step forward, but I just keep going. No medicine is strong enough… except Shawn. Shawn Davis.

"Chester will drive my car and we will take yours," he says.

"Where are we going?" I ask him because we are not on our way to either of our homes.

"To relax," he says simply. I choose not to argue.

Eventually, we reach the sea. Shawn stops the car.

"Beach? You're crazy, it's cold!"

"You should sing a song titled 'Shawn is Crazy'," observes Shawn and I roll my eyes. "Just come."

"You don't want to drown me, do you?" I ask him, squinting my eyes as he laughs.

"That is the reason why I drove all this way. Of course!" he says ironically. I don't want to get cold so I just stay in the car.

Shawn gets out and walks round to my side. "Come on, you are so stubborn," he groans.

I pout and cross my arms. "I agree. Now let's go somewhere warmer." He opens the door and just lifts me out. "Shawn! What are you doing? Shawn let go of me or I will kill you," I threaten as he chuckles.

"My biggest dream is to die by your hands baby," he mocks and smirks.

He puts me down on the sand and I frown, I turn away. Shawn is facing my back; I just feel like playing the baby today.

"You got your period or what?" he groans behind me.

I roll my eyes. He is a teeny-tiny bit annoyed. When I turn to him and smile, he is eyeing me as if I were a demon. He rolls his eyes and then we walk along the beach. There is no one around here, it's calm and relaxing. We sit under a tree; Shawn's arm is wrapped around my shoulder.

"Watching the ocean can calm you down sometimes, you know?" he says as I watch the regular rhythm of the waves.

"I guess," I sigh and wrap my arms around my knees.

"Do you want... to talk about it?" he asks nervously, and I shake my head.

"I'm fine."

"You know that one day you will have to tell me everything, don't you?"

"Yes, I know," I sigh. "Just not now."

"All right. So, we're going to use this time in another way," he whispers against my ear and I shiver. My fit of crying this morning seems a long time ago. When Shawn is around, I'm fine, too fine. He turns my face to him and plunges his gaze into mine, communicating to me all his care and affection. He kisses me slowly and then faster and more passionately. I lie down on the sand. He moves on top of me, holding his weight with his elbows. He kisses my neck, my face and around the curves of my breasts. He makes me feel good, physically and emotionally.

"You don't know how important you are to me," he whispers, his voice is shaking with the pleasure growing inside him. He takes the lobe of my ear between his teeth and bites it gently; a groan escapes my mouth and I feel him smile against me. I know that if we don't stop now, this will go too far and I'm not sure I want that. He stops it for me and lies down next to me, my hand in his. The sand is uncomfortable, but I don't really care, only Shawn matters, he and I, we, us, together.

He stands up and gives me his hand. I take it and stand up. We walk to the ocean and stand by the sea. A first wave wets our feet, the cold and delicious water massages my feet; I chew on my bottom lip and close my eyes to enjoy the moment. The sun is already saying goodbye. When Shawn goes back to work (from which he took vacation), we won't have enough of those moments any more. The night has always been my dark time, the moment I go to my room, in my bed to cry. But I just want it to be calm this time, to be peaceful and not harmful. I want to open my heart and pour my worries and my demons into this water. Let it take them far away from me. My hand is in Shawn's. We look at each other and smile. His messy hair is moving and mine is flying, his cheeks are red because of the cold.

"When I was little, my parents and I used to go to the beach. We loved it in our family. Each time I was feeling bad, my mom told me to remember the waves. Sometimes they're calm and slow but sometimes they're more violent and fast. But still, they get to their destination, even if it's not by the same route," says Shawn with feeling. I wish I had met Shawn's parents. I would have loved to know what they were like, how Shawn was before they died. I wish he had never had to endure such a terrible experience.

We are now closer to the water, I bend down and scope water into my cupped hands and throw it at Shawn, I chuckle.

"You want to play?" he says playfully and I smell something bad coming.

I run along the beach in the water with Shawn behind me, we are both laughing. "How can you be that fast today?" he asks behind me and I giggle, running faster. The Saturday's running is doing me good.

"You are the one who forces me to jog every Saturday, so you take responsibility," I shout and laugh more. I don't know how, but he suddenly wraps his arms around me and catches me against his chest. I try to escape but he is too strong.

"It's wrong. Students will never overtake their teacher," he whispers sensually in my ear. I feel my legs shaking.

Shawn turns to walk to the car, he stumbles and we fall in the water. At the same moment, a big wave crashes over us. The water fills my ears, my mouth, my nose and my eyes. It's painful but funny. We quickly stand up laughing and leave the cold water before we freeze. I don't get why the weather is so cold these days. He puts his arms around my waist and I lean against his chest. I am shaking because of the cold. We slowly walk to the car while Shawn makes some ridiculous jokes about the beach. Fortunately, I have some blankets in my car so we swaddle ourselves tightly. Shawn kisses me before we get in the car.

CHAPTER FOURTEEN

"Seriously?" my mother asks, eyeing me as if I were an apparition.

"Sure, I think it's a good idea," I answer simply and shrug.

"So you aren't going to make us beg you or anything?" my father continues, seriously surprised.

I try to hide my amusement. "If you guys keep on like this, I will seriously think about saying no," I threaten. "I'm just done refusing to have fun with my family," I add quietly; the light in their eyes is a hopeful one. They are starting to believe that I will return to my old self. Their happy and lovely girl. Before I used to find any excuse to not hang out with them. During my depression, it was easier because no one really wanted to hang out with a depressive person.

"I'll call Shawn to ask him then," I say before heading to the living room.

***

In the evening, my parents and I are dressed for family dinner. I'm a bit worried that Shawn will come without Frida. I haven't seen her in a while and I really miss her. I am wearing a strapless blue dress that comes a little above my knees, accompanied by a pair of black pumps. I put on light makeup.

"Someone wants to drive someone crazy," my mother teases, and she winks. Father and I roll our eyes.

The doorbell rings and I quickly walk to open it. Shawn is wearing a blue tee and chinos with black converse and a jacket. His hair is neatly combed, making him look serious. I bet that by the time we arrive at the restaurant, it will be a total mess — the messy hair I love. His eyes scan me up and down. If he could, he would have jumped on me. I chuckle at the thought. Since when am I so free in my mind?

"Wow, you look wonderfully blue!" he jokes and compliments me.

"So, do you," I reply with a wink.

"Good evening Mr and Mrs Lawson," Shawn says with the angelic voice he uses to talk to older people. "Thank you for inviting me. My grandma preferred to wait in the car."

"No problem. We're really glad to have the whole family together," my dad says, and I blush. So, they consider Shawn like a family member, a part of our family. How? Like my future husband and their future son-in-law, then the future father of my children, and so the one who'll kill cockroaches in my house? I mentally slap myself for thinking about marriage after two months of a relationship.

"Shawn, can we talk to you in private?" Mom suddenly asks and panic runs inside me.

"Why? What are you going to tell him?" I hastily ask.

"None of your business, darling" replies my mother through a smile. I roll my eyes impudently.

"Sure, no problem," Shawn answers. He doesn't even look nervous. What kind of boyfriend can be calm before a private talk with his girlfriend's parents? Shawn, I guess. None of my business. I am sure she is going to talk about me.

I sit on the couch and patiently wait for them, but my curiosity is pushing me to listen to the conversation. I stand up and walk quietly to the kitchen and stand by the door.

"You really don't have to thank me for that. I am the one who is thankful to know your daughter," Shawn says.

"Seriously. We are very grateful to you for coming into her life and making her happy."

"She is just as important for me," he says kindly. I accidentally kick the table by me and a glass of water my mother had left on it falls, but I catch it quickly, breathing loudly.

"Do you love her?" Dad suddenly asks and the glass falls from my hands, but once again I catch it. A moment of silence fills the kitchen and my heart sinks. I thought mother was clumsy but how could Dad ask that! "I mean; we really don't want you to hurt her. She's fragile. She can't take any more hurt. I promised myself that I'll break the bones of any boy coming around her. But you seem good for her so please, don't hurt her." I want to be angry with him for telling Shawn that I am fragile, for confirming that I made them suffer all the time I was depressed but the love they're showing me holds me back from being angry.

"I won't dare. She has also changed my life even though she doesn't realize it and I'm really fond of her." I am not sure my heart can take more. This is so beautiful. As I don't hear anything more, I peek inside and see all of them smiling. Oh, they are coming back. I quickly look around, grab one of my father's books and jump on the couch, acting like I was reading. They all come in and I smile to them.

"Hope you had a good talk," I say, looking at the book even though I am not actually seeing anything, because Shawn's sentence is echoing in my mind. *I am really fond of her.* Does he love me? No, it would be too fast. But then, someone once told me, love doesn't know time. You can love someone to your bones after meeting them a second ago, the difficulty is staying in love and making it real.

"I will get my jacket," my mother says before leaving the living room.

Shawn bends down and whispers in my ear, "The book is upside down."

I blush and throw a quick look at it. I turn it round. I close it hastily and smile uncomfortably to Shawn who is making fun of me and shaking his head. We finally leave the house in my father's car. I sit at the back with Frida and Shawn. My parents love her; my mother even invites her to an event at the hospital for older women.

"Those were the good old days," Frida says to my parents as they laugh at her stories about her young days. She says that all the boys were running after her. She finally chose the one who was always clowning around to make her laugh: Shawn's grandfather. I glance at Shawn and we smile to each other. I love this, this moment.

We finally arrive at the restaurant called "Funny Food". I am nervous at seeing the name of the restaurant. Which kind of funny foods are they serving here? Shawn tenses as we arrive. He is odd since when my father said that we were coming here.

"Are you okay or don't you like the restaurant?" I ask him, frowning.

"No, it's fine," he stammers.

We walk in and many waiters are looking at us, smiling. I am helping Frida even though she has her cane. I don't know what is going on here.

"Hey Shawn; long time, no see. You've not come here for so long. Where is Mia?" a waiter asks him.

"She's fine. I have been busy," he answers nervously.

Mia? Who is Mia? How do they all know him around here? We sit at a table and Shawn looks away.

"Do you like the place? My colleagues always talk about it," my mother says.

I was so concentrated on Shawn's behavior that I hadn't noticed how beautiful the place is. All the tables have different colors and patterns. The walls are high and made of glass and the ceiling is wonderfully decorated. The waiters are wearing colorful clothes. I would rename this restaurant "The Colorful Foods". There is a big podium in one corner of the restaurant. There's a group doing a funny song and dance routine.

We order, but during the dinner Shawn is terribly quiet and absent.

"Ladies and gentlemen, welcome Tipsy the clown," a voice says into a microphone and everyone applauds as if they have been waiting for him since they arrived. Shawn's face goes darker. What is going on?

"This was Mia's favorite moment," Frida says gloomily, staring at an invisible point. Obviously, she can't see anything.

My parents are too concentrated on their conversation to notice anything. A clown appears in the room. He tells some jokes that are actually really good. It feels like déjà vu, because I am sure that I have heard some of the jokes before, from Shawn. Shawn stands up suddenly. "I'm going to the washroom," he stammers into his beard.

He walks by the clown who seems to recognize him, but Shawn ignores him and walks faster. After dinner, when we arrive home, Mom and Dad go into the house after the goodbyes, but I stay with Shawn and Frida. "Do you still want to do that movie night?" I ask Frida.

"Of course."

"I don't think this is the right time, Grandma is tired," Shawn interjects, rubbing the back of his head.

"I'm not," she replies and Shawn sighs.

"Just give me five minutes," I say.

I quickly enter the house, put on some comfortable clothes and rejoin them. We silently drive to theirs. Shawn is really quiet. We wait in the kitchen while he gets changed.

"Do you know what's wrong with him tonight?" I ask Frida and she gives me a sad smile after taking a sip of her herbal tea.

"That restaurant was the favorite one of Mia, his sister."

I blench and frown. Sister? Shawn has never told me he has or had a sister. What is the story?

"Wh-what happened?" I ask.

"It's weird that he hasn't talked to you about her," she says.

I start feeling a heavy weight on my heart, lost in my thoughts.

"I'm ready."

I turn to Shawn. His eyes are red as if he is holding himself back from crying.

"Excuse me, Frida. Shawn, can I talk to you?"

He hesitates but finally sighs. "Sure."

We walk to his room. He sits at the foot of his bed and invites me to join him, but I don't really want to sit. I just stand in front of him.

"Why didn't you tell me about your sister? Where is she?" I snap.

After a long moment of silence, he answers. "In a grave." The way he says it makes me shiver.

"I... I'm sorry. What happened to her?"

He looks away and then back at me as if he's afraid of telling me the truth. As if he is hiding something from me. I put my discomfort aside and kneel down between his legs and gently stroke his cheek, looking into his eyes.

"Talk to me please," I beg. My voice is strangely broken.

I've never seen him this way before. I never thought that Shawn would be sad. I was making a mistake everyone makes nowadays. We think happy people are never sad. I forgot that even someone with the brightest smile has his dark moments.

"I was very close to her. She was just three years younger than me. We were a kind of perfect family," he starts quietly. He tries to speak again but sobs are threatening to take over him. He shakes his head as if he wanted to remove all its contents. He walks to the window and runs his hand through his hair. "I should have seen it, I should have seen all that was happening to her," he moans.

He finally turns on me. "She was bullied in school because she was very underdeveloped for her age. They made fun of her. People think their jokes about people's look are just jokes but they don't know how much it hurts. She was hiding it from us. She was acting as if she were completely happy. But one day, she couldn't handle it any more. She told me to drive her to the pharmacy and she made me stay in the car. I thought it was for women's stuff because she was thirteen." He closes his eyes as if he were living the scene again, then opens them.

CHAPTER FIFTEEN

"I didn't know I was driving her to buy poison. When we got back home, she hugged me and told me she loved me..." Shawn stops and runs his hand over his face. He is still holding himself from crying, the veins on his forehead are throbbing.

"The next time I saw her, she was in her bed, dead. The rat poison on the nightstand," he adds quietly. "I'd never noticed anything; can you just imagine it? She had all the symptoms, but I never noticed them. My parents felt guilty. My mother especially, for giving birth to a disabled child and she just never woke up the day after Mia's burial. My father followed months later." Shawn leans against the wall, as if he can't stand up straight any more.

"I don't know how I let all that happen. I tried to be strong for them, but they all gave up. That's why I decided to become psychologist; that's why I chose happiness over sadness; that's why I'm the Shawn you know."

I stay quiet throughout his speech, wordless. This is a terrible story and I feel terribly sorry for him, for Mia and their whole family.

"Shawn..." I start quietly and walk slowly to him. "You know that it's not your fault, don't you? I'm sure she is proud of you for keeping fighting. Because now you're helping people. You helped me."

"That's what I thought I could do, but I know you're still depressed and, like her, you're trying to hide it."

Evidence flashes in my mind and I recoil, refusing to think about it. I nervously shake my head as if the thought would leave it.

"You... you talked to me because you thought that I would do what she did? You approached me out of pity and fear? You..." My eyes go wide and I back away again. "No... Shawn." My eyes are hurting me and tears are welling up. I don't want to believe it. He walks over to me.

"No, Fifa, please, I really like you."

I quickly pull my wrist from his hold and back away again, shaking my head. "I thought you really liked me. You're with me just for that? Because you don't want me to die, like her? You think, you really think that I could? You see your sister through me?" Then all pieces of the puzzles fall into place in front of me. I remember his question from when we met: Why do you look so sad?

"No, never. I swear." He looks down, bites his bottom lip and looks back at me, confused. "Yes, in the beginning, I mean, your first year. I noticed all the symptoms and I wanted to help you, but when I really met you, everything changed. I started to have feelings for you."

I shake my head. "You're lying, Shawn."

"I'm not incestuous, I wouldn't go as far as dating you because of that," he tries to convince me, his voice much louder and desperate.

Tears are falling onto my cheeks and an incredible pain grows in my heart. One of the only things I thought was real is just fake, an illusion. I've just been his way of relieving his conscience. My whole body is shaking. I blink several times, to wake up from this nightmare. Everywhere I look it's written "no one really cares about you."

I run away from him, sprinting down the stairs and out of the house. Shawn is running behind me and begging, but I don't listen, the pain is growing and growing. This is showing me how important he is to me, even though I'm not really important to him, but I know how much he is suffering, how hard I want to hug him and make him forget the past. The same way he helped me. But it is over.

"Please, Fifa," he grabs my wrist and turns me to him, he's shaking. "Please, don't go."

It takes a big effort to pull my wrist away, not just because he is much stronger than me, but because I don't want to stay away from him. I want to come back, to trust him, but then again, I remember. Shawn pities me, he sees me like a future patient. And all the pain comes back, and I tear my wrist from his hold.

"Don't you dare to follow me," I scream so hard that my vocal cords pain me. He is paralyzed. I run and run and run. I run as if hell were behind and hunting me. I've never run so hard. Tears all falling and falling, and my chest is hurting and hurting. It's over.

I enter the house, slamming the door behind me before I remember that my parents are around. I run to my room, this time shutting the door quietly to not wake my parents up. I slide down the door to sit, back against it. I cry and cry and cry but the pain is growing and growing. It's so painful that I can feel it physically. Shawn considers me as a patient with problems not his girlfriend. I put my hand against my mouth to cry in silence and I lie on the floor, till I fall asleep. I am tired of suffering... maybe I should do what Mia did. Did she feel better after? I think that's why many people commit suicide. They think that the pain will leave them, they think that they won't have to suffer any more. But what if... what if the pain doesn't leave? What if it is much stronger afterwards?

I miss Shawn. I want him with me. I want him for me; I want him to really care for me. But he doesn't. And the worse is that I am falling in love with him. His cologne, his scent is on me. Why is it so difficult to be happy, to just live? Are the dead happier? Are they all making fun of those of us who are still living? But the most painful things is, that I am really like Mia. It is also because of bullies that I became depressed.

***

My whole body is paining me when I wake up on Sunday. I am still lying on the floor and I can barely move my neck. What stopped me from getting into bed, just a few feet from the door? Maybe I wanted to suffer more. Masochism. I stand up too quickly, and the pain in my head increases and the room spins around me. I feel like giants are jumping in my head. I breathe deeply, my hands over my face, but regret it as soon as the smell of my breath hits my nose. If I were married right now, I could kill my husband with it when we woke up. I smile at my joke and think that I am sure Shawn would have loved it and my mood falls again.

I stand in front of the mirror to analyze my face: my eyes are swollen and red, my lips chapped and my nose is reddish. I head to the bathroom and brush my teeth before I risk killing either of my parents; and then I slowly walk to the kitchen. My parents are in their Sunday best, but their gazes are puzzled as soon as they see me.

"Good morning," I say with a fake smile.

"Hi," my mother says quietly, frowning.

"Morning!" Father says.

I know they are silently fighting about who will ask what's wrong with me, who will take the risk of being squashed.

"Where are you guys going?" I ask casually, at least, I hope it came out that way.

"Church," Father answers.

My parents are devout Christians, especially my father. We pray before eating and he always goes to church when he can, at least once a week. Mother has less time with her work as a doctor. I don't have strong faith but throughout those years I was deeply feeling alone, I knelt down and started talking to God and I felt heard and listened to and it was a good feeling.

"Can I go?" I ask them and they frown before nodding.

I walk to the pantry, but the shelf is too high and I am too short. I have to stretch before even managing to touch the cereal box. I wonder who put it there. I hit the wood angrily and groan, "Stupid cereal. Get down here."

My parents are looking at each other behind me, in dismay, still uncomfortable with not knowing what's going on with me. But I know they know it has something to do with Shawn. Just yesterday, they literally begged him to not hurt me. Nevertheless, he did hurt me, or I am the one who hurt him, or we simply hurt each other. The problem is that he hurt me in a good way, with good intentions, while I just wanted to say harsh words to him.

"I don't think the pantry has done anything bad to you, let me help you," Father says and stands up, but I turn on him.

"Don't. I'm not a baby any more, am I?" I say frostily and he sits back down.

Normally, my father would never let me speak to him this way, but he is just afraid of me being depressed again. Maybe is he afraid of me killing myself? I push the thought from my mind and sigh.

"Sorry Dad."

"Don't worry."

I turn back to the pantry and finally manage to grab the box after a few minutes of fighting and sit. My father's phone rings and he stands to take the call in the living room, saying it was a colleague. I feel my mother's gaze on me, and I am avoiding meeting her gaze, no matter what.

"What did he do?" she finally asks, making me glance at her.

"Who?" I ask looking away, even though I know perfectly well that she's talking about Shawn.

"Fifa?" she insists, staring at me and I sigh.

"I just thought he really cared for me."

I'm not sure it will be respectful to talk about his sister to anyone. Maybe he trusts me enough to tell me the whole story. But does he really or was it just a part of his plan to get me out of my depression?

"Doesn't he? I would have bet he does."

I roll my eyes and giggle nervously because if I don't laugh, I will cry.

"He just approached me because he knew that I was not feeling well in my life... In my head," I add lower. Said like that, it seems the best thing that someone who cares for you could do, but at the same time it sounds so insane.

"And you think because of that he doesn't love you? I mean, doesn't care about you?" she asks me in a very soft tone. I'm just thinking about the best way to get out of this conversation.

"Nothing is even real with me except bad things," I sigh and look down at my wet cereal.

"I think you shouldn't let your ego talk for you but your heart," Mother says, leaning against the kitchen counter.

"You think this is ego?" My voice is much louder than I want it to be. "You think that getting hurt by someone you thought really cared for you is ego? You think that being hurt because someone you thought liked who you really are, just saw you as a charity case, that's ego? So, okay, I'm really proud," I exclaimed, swinging my arms in all directions.

I try to control myself, but this is much more difficult than I thought it would be. It was much easier years ago to control everything, how I felt, to show what I wanted to show.

"I don't mean it like that and you know it," she starts, pointing at me. "I just think Shawn is right for you. You looked so happy with him." I don't know why but her words hurt me, or I really do know why. Tears are gathering in my eyes and I stand up, shaking.

"So that's it? Huh? You just don't want me to become again that depressed and annoying daughter I've always been?" I watch how silent she is and shake my head. "Yes, you're just afraid of having a drag around you, aren't you?" I hiss, looking at her with hurt and dark eyes. I am so relieved that father is not back to the kitchen yet. I am sure he has started working. I don't feel strong enough to face the two of them. My mother runs her hand through her hair and sighs, but I don't give up. "If that's it, don't worry. I'll just leave and go far, very far, to Australia maybe. Then you won't have to see me any more. I'll send you pictures and messages showing that I'm happy. After all, thousands of people are faking their happiness in this world." I stop talking to catch my breath; my chest is rising and falling. My mother looks hurt but doesn't say anything. I run my shaking hand through my hair.

"I'm sorry, Mom," I apologize in a whisper. She's still silent, looking at me with sympathetic eyes. I hesitantly walk to her and throw my arms around her for a hug. I miss those old days, when I just hugged my mother at any opportunity. Her sweet and maternal perfume used to calm me and still does. She hugs me hard and I sob. "I don't want it again; I want to be happy. Why did Shawn do that? Why can't I just skip it?" This is the first time I'm so open with her and it feels terribly good to talk to the woman who gave birth to me, who suffered for me and who loves me. She strokes my hair gently, as she used to do before. "I think we went too fast," I whisper hoping that she'll break her silence.

"I don't think so. You're just two young people who don't know how to handle problems," she says. That's right about me, but for Shawn I'm not sure it is. But I just shut up to listen to her lovely voice. I'm nineteen, but here I am crying in my mother's arms like a baby. Yet, this is so comfortable. "Give yourself some time, okay?" she says, and I nod and lean more into her chest.

"I love you, Mom," I whisper, and I feel her smile.

"I love you, darling."

***

The service was good, and I don't regret going to church today. I loved the gospel songs and the words of God. The pastor talked about forgiveness. I felt like God specially set it up for me today, to hear them. He said that it's difficult and hard, but we have to forgive the people who hurt us, because we hurt God everyday with our sins. Yet, he always forgives us. I think I should just forgive

Shawn, but sometimes I need to put things straight in my head. Back from church, the three of us watch Tom and Jerry in the living room with drinks and plenty of popcorns. I love it. To start with, I don't really laugh, so father tickles me mercilessly, and I laugh so much that I fall off the couch. Then we all burst into laughter.

In the evening, after working, I sit by my window. Now that I have let Shawn sit here, I can't stop feeling his presence by me, smiling to me, kissing me. My phone rings and I secretly hope that it is him, but it is Caroline. Maybe was I right about the fact that Shawn has never cared for me the way I thought he did. I clear my throat and pick up with a smile even though she can't see me.

"Hi Fifa, what's up? We were with Shawn today and you weren't there," she says and a stupid question leaves my mouth.

"With Shawn? How was he?" I don't know why I am asking that, she may suspect that something is wrong. "I mean how was it? The stuff you were doing... I mean whatever you guys were doing..." I try to backtrack but make it worse.

"Well... he was normal." This hurts me. He is normal while I am almost dead. *You are so dramatic,* my consciousness grumbles. "I mean normal Shawn who smiles all the time without really letting any of his feelings show," she adds.

"Now that I think about it, he didn't really look okay. Did you guys have a fight or something? Because you don't seem okay either." I realize that's not Caroline's voice and that Kate's there too.

"Hello, Kate. Um..." I don't know what to say. "Just random stuff, don't worry," I lie even though they will figure everything out one day.

"If you say so. Wednesday we're going to do some shopping. You should come with us," Caroline says. That's really nice of them. I smile.

"Sure, I'd love to." *As long as there is no Shawn.*

"Great. Have a lovely night. Mwah, love that we are friends now'," they say at the same time. I find it really funny.

"Thank you, girls. Same to you."

And we hang up, and I am alone once again. I really should learn to have fun myself and not always be waiting for other people. I think about it for a while. I scan the room to look for what I can do. I love to dance and I have not danced for a while. I put on some music and dance and sing... alone. With "There's Nothing Holding Me Back" by Shawn Mendes, I feel like a bird, flying in the sky, free and crazy. I jump all around the room and try to get all this stress out of me. I should send this to Shawn. Fifa's tip for happiness: Do something stupid or dance like shit. I chuckle at the thought, but mentally slap myself for thinking about Shawn again. I fall onto the bed with a deep sigh. I take a quick shower and slowly fall asleep, Shawn's photo displayed on my screen.

CHAPTER SIXTEEN

*H*appiness *tip eight: Face your problems. Please let's just talk.*

When I read Shawn's text, I let out a relieved sigh. That tip is specific to our situation. But even if we talk, what are we going to talk about? About me jumping in his arms and just forgetting all that happened? About him confessing that he just saw me as he dead sister whom he finally got the chance to save? I don't know if I am strong enough to bear it, to feel his gaze on me. I have chosen him over Dylan and Hailey because I thought he was a real person in my life. Besides, I don't even want to be friends with them any more, not just because of Shawn.

Dressed in midnight blue dungarees, a white long-sleeve shirt and my sneakers, I walk into the hallway of my faculty, praying to not meet Shawn. I rush to reach my philosophy class even though it's too early. I am one of the least lucky people in the world because right now, there is not only Shawn and Chester on the way, but also Dylan and Hailey. A diabolical thought crosses my mind that I could join Dylan and Hailey to piss Shawn off, but that would just humiliate me. I lower my head and walk quickly.

"Hey, Fifa," Chester calls loudly as usual. I just want to bury myself under the building. "Fifa, are you deaf?" he calls louder still. I want to slap him, because I am sure he knows about Shawn and me. Everyone is staring at

111

me. "Fifaaaa," he continues, and I suddenly turn and walk quickly to him, gripping the straps of my backpack tightly. If I were not too pissed off, I would find his outfit very funny — he is wearing 80s style pink pants, which are too tight, with a purple T-shirt that is too big and the highlight of the show, platform shoes. Like, what goes on in his mind when he gets dressed? I struggle with all my strength to look angry and not amused.

"What, Chester?" I snap, forcing myself to look threatening. I stare at him too intensely so as not to look at Shawn who is nearby. I can feel Shawn's gaze on me. He is leaning against the wall, silently, wearing a navy shirt and black jeans. I am sure he is looking hot, but I can't dare to look at him.

"Well, you just walked past us," Chester says simply, arms crossed and eyes crinkled.

"Gee, I didn't see you," I lie, looking at my feet.

"You did and I had to call you several times. How can you not greet your boyfriend and your brother-in-law?" Oh my God, I'll kill him. I breathe slowly to control myself and to forget the pain that appears in my chest when he says boyfriend. Chester can't hold his tongue; he just says whatever comes to his mind.

"I... I don't know what you're talking about," I reply defensively.

"You do."

I roll my eyes. "Just let me go to class, Chester. I don't feel like playing," I sigh and he keeps silent. He might have understood that this time, the funny and stupid things are not going to work. I know that I shouldn't avoid Shawn. I know that he is just waiting for me to speak to him, because he doesn't know if he has the right to talk to me. However, my mother is right; I am too proud to just let it go.

I walk straight to my class and sit at my usual place. Maybe Shawn won't dare to sit next to me; I don't want to be the only one avoiding contact. I lower my head and try to read my notes before the class starts. Minutes later, Shawn arrives in the class and looks around. I know because I am showing some of my notes to the girl behind me. She thanks me with a smile, and I turn back to my notes. My heart is pounding too fast. He sits next to me; I can't believe it. I just keep looking at my notes, cursing myself for coming this early.

"You look nice today."

I struggle to not look too relieved that he tries to speak to me, and I turn to him with a normal look, despite the fact that I am surely shaking. "Thanks," I almost whisper.

"You... you still don't want to talk about it?" he says hesitantly. I am sure that because I thanked him, he thinks that he can continue talking and that I may agree to talk with him. And there again, it is the right thing to do, talk about the problems and resolve them, not avoid them. But I never do the right thing. I keep silent and he sighs. "Please. I can't bear this situation. And you're not even speaking to me. I need you to speak to me," he begs and I just want to jump on him right now and kiss him, and talk to him, and hug him. Why is it sometimes so hard to do what we want to do?

I am so relieved when the lecturer enters the room. For the rest of the day, I avoid Shawn. I have lunch in a quiet place of the school, far from the cafeteria. He starts to call and text me and I feel more and more guilty.

Fifa where are you? Is everything fine?

I know I fucked up, but please just give me a chance to fix it? I miss you.

I am sorry for what Chester did.

Fifa! Please.

I finally switch my phone off to stop myself from reading any more of them, to just not increase my pain. Tuesday, it is the same thing. But today, we have to go to the O.V. club. I can't skip such an important activity because of my personal problems. I head to the club, hoping that Shawn won't notice me, and also hoping the total opposite. There are not that many people in the club and the room has been arranged with tables around. Before, we have just talked about how to manage things and the associations we are going to help. Once, with Shawn and Chester, we agreed to drive to the other side of the province to give some school things to the orphans. It was lovely and Shawn and Chester even made up a dance for them to do.

I sit at a table. Shawn enters right after me. He glances at me, sadness filling his eyes and I want to call him over, but someone does it before me and I think it is just better that way. "Shawn, come here," a stunning redhead girl calls him. He walks to her and sits.

Throughout the meeting, my eyes are on them. She smiles a lot, not like me. And they are really enjoying themselves and joking about. I sigh and focus on the letter I'm writing. We each met an orphan and we are sending him or her letters. I met Charly, a really amazing Korean boy. He lost both parents at the same time, but he is struggling so that they would be proud of him. I don't have to struggle to find the words to tell him how special he is. I wish him a bright and great future, because he deserves it and all the orphans do. I don't know what I would have done if I didn't have my parents with me. I don't tell them enough but their love and patience really helped me.

***

It is hard to have someone you want to talk to in front of you, but to not be able to talk to him. It is so hard that everything is so hard.

"Hello," Kate greets me with a warm smile before hugging me.

"Baby F," Caroline says, kissing me on both cheeks and I chuckle. I love these girls.

"Ready for a super-cool shopping day?" Kate asks me and I nod shyly.

We get in their car and head to the mall. Once there, Kate is already pulling me to a shop. "I saw such a nice top that will perfectly fit you," she squeals.

"Hi baby," Caroline says to a girl and they do air kisses - like London in The Suite Life of Zack and Cody, and the girl also greets Kate.

"Who is this beautiful girl?" the girl asks, looking at me with a smile.

"This is Fifame, our friend. Fifa this is Genevieve, the owner of this shop," Kate says.

Now that I look around, I notice signs in French. This is a French shop for sure. *Chez G* is the name. We walk around the place and the two sisters keep throwing clothes to me.

Caroline suddenly turns to me. "Now you can try them on," she says and I silently head to the fitting room.

The dress I try is a white dress slightly slinky that shows my curves and comes above the knees, my shoulders are bare and the sleeves are long. I exhale and walk shyly out.

Only Kate is sitting there and her eyes light up as soon as she sees me.

"Oh my God, you're so gorgeous. Look at those curves!," she rhapsodizes and I blush.

"Look who just joined us."

I turn my head to the left and meet Shawn's gaze and my mouth literally falls open. Caroline is pushing him to sit. She's holding a fruit juice with the mall logo. Shawn's eyes are on me, too intense, as if he were scanning my body.

"Look at this sexy girlfriend you have," Caroline says, looking at me. Shawn hasn't told them about us, but did we even break up? I look down.

"Shawn, what do you think about this?" Kate asks as he scratches his temple.

He clears his throat, uncomfortable, and looks into my eyes. I can't look away; my eyes are glued on him. "She is... wow," he answers, his cheeks turning pink.

"Shawn says you look wow, so you'll take it," Kate decides and I roll my eyes but smile. "And we're sorry if you came for other stuff. But you have to look for clothes for your girlfriend instead. Not meaning that she doesn't have any clothes, but she has a great shape. She has to try new styles."

I've never seen someone so into my shape and it's surprising me. I don't really think that I am as sexy as she says. I walk back to the fitting room. I take more time to prepare myself to face Shawn once more. I'm wearing a black leather strapless playsuit that comes to the middle of my thighs. I am not really comfortable in this one.

"Oh God!" Shawn exclaims when I come out of the changing room.

"I think this one is... too much, too sexy" I say in a low voice to the girls.

"Definitely," Shawn agrees, the mouth open and breathing hardly.

"Okay, okay, but you're so sexy. You can wear it... you know... just for Shawn," Caroline says with so much suggestiveness that I almost choke on my saliva. How can she talk like that? My eyes meet Shawn's and we shyly smile to each other, both at the mercy of the twins. I actually love having him around.

***

After a whole afternoon of shopping, and hands full of bags, we head to a restaurant inside the mall. They are serving African foods, because for the first time, I choose the restaurant. Shawn and I glance at each other throughout the dinner, but no one talks except the twins who are talking about their art courses. Shawn finally suggests driving me home. I think about rejecting the offer but I just agree. The drive is silent. When he finally stops at my house driveway, he turns off the engine. I know he wants to talk and I start to panic. I quickly get out without letting him speak.

"Night, Shawn," I shout and literally run to the house.

I watch him through the window. He looks at the house for a long time but finally sighs and leaves. When I turn round, my eyes land on my parents who are looking at me with curious expressions. I smile nervously.

"Hi, goodnight," I quickly say and run to my room.

At bedtime, I go on Instagram. Shawn has posted photos of us from the last few weeks. We looked so happy. I stay lying on the bed, eyes on the ceiling and thinking about Shawn, again and again. The way he acted today, blushing and so careful. The way I am acting like a dummy with him. I sigh deeply. What am I so afraid of?

CHAPTER SEVENTEEN

I write down my name on the list of candidates. Everyone is laughing at me. "You're just a shitty short black girl." "Move." "We don't want you." I am too thin, too small, too puny. My parents are looking at me and crying. Dark arms are pulling me into a hole, and I am shouting and screaming, but no one saves me. I am in a tomb and my family is crying.

***

I wake up suddenly, sweaty with messy hair. My chest is heavy, my heart is pounding. Tears are falling on my cheeks which are burning. I am trying to convince myself that it was just a nightmare, nothing more, nothing less. My hands are shaking as I grab my phone and automatically call Shawn. I don't know why, but I just want him to help me. He picks up after the third ring.

"Fifa?" he says in surprise. His voice is tired because I just woke him up. I keep the phone against my ear while he is still saying my name, but I can't speak, my body is shaking. I hang up and lie back on the bed.

He calls me straight back and I hesitate but pick up. "Fifa, are you okay?" he asks, worry filling his voice. *Talk to him, please*, my consciousness begs me.

"Shawn," I say in a whisper; a sob escapes my throat. I clap my hand against my mouth to stop it, but the more I hold it in, the more I want to cry.

"Fifa? Please tell me what's wrong. Do you want me to come over?" he begs. Would he really come to my house at this hour? I don't care whether it is because he's afraid for me, or that I might do something stupid. All that matters is that Shawn cares for me.

"Shawn, I can't..." I say, crying.

"You can't what?" he asks.

"I... nightmare," I sigh and wipe the tears from my face.

"What was it? Tell me."

I don't want to talk about it. I don't even want to continue this conversation; I don't want him to pity me again. I inhale deeply and sigh, "Goodnight Shawn." I hang up.

I can't get back to sleep; my eyes are wide open. I stay awake for the rest of the night, too afraid to face those nightmares again. I get out of bed around four a.m. to go for a jog. When I come out, Shawn is sitting in front of the house.

I quickly turn to go back in but he speaks, "Come on, wait."

I slowly turn to him. "I'm not here to beg you again for forgiveness. I just want to check on you," he explains softly.

We are heading towards the month of November and the weather is very cold. My nostrils are kind of frozen and paining me. Shawn's nose is red, mine is only slightly red because of my brown skin. He slowly comes closer to me and strokes my cheek, staring at me. This is so good. I missed his fingers against my skin. I let him do it because I don't even want to resist any more.

"Talk to me, what was the nightmare?"

I look away and remove his hand from my face. My skin complains at my betrayal.

"Shawn," I sigh.

"This is silly. We can't just stop talking to each other. I need you and I want you near me," he laments and a tear falls on my cheek.

"But you don't care for me the way I do for you, and this is hurting me," I confess and a weight leaves my heart.

He turns my face to him before burying his gaze in mine. "You're wrong. I really like you, I can't even stop thinking about you. You're now part of me, Fifa," he says in a whisper. Our foreheads are glued to each other, and we feel each other's breath on our faces.

"I… I'm just tired of everyone's pity. I don't want you to do all that because of my… you know."

"Honestly, I don't want to lie to you." He moves his head back but leaves his hands on my face. "I hate seeing you sad. But I'm not doing all this because of that. I'm doing it because you mean a lot to me. Not as a sister but as a woman." And in a really slow and sensual voice he adds, "A really beautiful and great woman." Shawn has no idea of how intimidating he can be, and how perfect.

I bite my bottom lip and then smile at him. "Okay, but let's just be friends first. We should learn more about each other. Let's go slow. Then you'll really know how you feel about me," I suggest and he smiles and removes his hands.

"I already know how I feel about you, but okay. As long as I'm with you and you talk to me. It's all right."

We smile to each other and hug. The hug has nothing to do with friendship' but it doesn't matter. His arms around my body, my head against his chest, his heart beating hard (I just want it to beat for me) and his wonderful scent wandering in my nostrils. Shawn smells particularly good for a man. I'm not saying that men smell bad, but Shawn smells better than anyone I know, even the women.

"Tell me, have you ever dated anyone before?" he finally asks when we get back from jogging.

"You mean like a real date?" I ask him, and he glares at me and I chuckle.

"I mean before me. Because we were dating. And we can continue to if you want to," he states.

I take a drink before answering. "Um yeah, but just one guy. He dumped me because of the state I was in. And I wasn't really into the relationship," I shrug. It was my junior year. Connor had been asking me out for years and I finally gave in because he was handsome and kind. However, I was not giving myself to it and he gave up. "What about you?"

"Well, yes. Two girls, but I was not really in love. I broke up with the second one when I first saw you in the university." My eyes go wide when he says it. "You could call me a stalker, but I was planning how to approach you and how to talk to you. But I think it was only because I liked you," he says and I blush.

"Stop, Shawn. Friends remember?" I tell him, trying to clean the grin on my face. He smirks.

"Shawn?"

Why does my mother always come into the kitchen when we are there? She is wearing her doctor's coat. She seems relieved to see Shawn around.

"Morning, Mrs Lawson."

She looks at me and I smile and then she talks to Shawn, "Very glad to see you around." And then she says, "Bye, I've got so many things to do today. And we're getting those new interns."

"I'm sure she thinks that we're back together," I tell Shawn as soon as she leaves.

"But you didn't tell her we weren't," he notes with a slight smile. I roll my eyes even though he is right.

"Huh, you're such an annoying boy," I whine.

"Then we match. You're just more annoying," he says and I chuckle. "I missed your smile so much," he adds and I roll my eyes to hide my happiness.

***

Happiness tip nine: There isn't really any tip for happiness. I told you, it's a choice.

"Chester Junior is around," Chester says in a really excited way and walks towards me.

I roll my eyes but smile at him. I am so glad to see them all. Today is Halloween; there is a big party around the campus, but we chose to meet just among ourselves. Chester is Scooby-Doo — he is even wearing a tail — Liam is Voldemort from Harry Potter. Liam's costume is by far the best here, he is even wearing makeup and has got the magic wand. Caroline is Janet Jackson; Kate is Hermione from Harry Potter; Tom is Lucky Luke with a fake gun. Shawn is ironically Shawn Mendes. He doesn't have a costume, but he did his hair like Shawn, and has fake tattoos which look like Shawn Mendes'. When I asked him who he was before noticing the tattoos, he told me the second Shawn I loved. I am Angelique Kidjo, a famous Beninese singer, my favorite one though. I made the effort of putting on a wig as Angelique's hair is cut very short and added some details only a real fan would notice. I think Shawn and I have the most random costumes here, but at least there is real story behind them.

"Ugh, I'm not Chester Junior. We have nothing in common," I say but hug him. Hugging Chester is so comfortable; it is like hugging a teddy bear. Both Chester and I run our hands through our hair (fake for me) and then down our neck after the hug while everyone is looking at us. That is weird; we do have some stuff in common. I smile, a little embarrassed. "Hello, guys."

"Hi Fifa," they say and Tom waves at me.

We are in a bar, but not the kind that's too loud. Okay maybe it is a teeny-tiny bit loud. It is a restaurant-bar. Okay, should I just shut up? I feel very high tonight. The music is so great and I just want to jump on the dancefloor and dance till the morning. I dance like shit. In nineteen years, I have only managed to master one dance: *Shaku shaku*, a Nigerian dance. But I don't care, I like to dance like shit. I chuckle while talking to myself as everyone stares at me with narrowed eyes. I jump from one foot to the other as I clear my throat.

We are all sitting. I am between Tom and Chester. Shawn is sitting in front of me. He looks so hot in that grey shirt with the first button open.

"So... you guys are now friends after being a couple?" Liam asks, a little confused like all the others except Chester who is devouring the amuse-bouches.

Shawn and I share look. I purse my lips, a little embarrassed, but we finally smile before nodding. We were actually dating when we first met and now we're friends; this is funny.

"Well, I don't even want to understand," Liam shrugs as the waiter brings the drinks we ordered before sitting. The place is not that crowded.

"The mojito is mine," I exclaim. They all look at me with surprise to which I shrug before drinking a long sip.

They're serving the drinks in small pumpkins. It is cool and so Halloween.

"You drink alcohol?" Tom signs and I roll my eyes.

"What do you guys think? That I'm a kind of holy virgin?" I ask, pouting, but they nod. "I wish I were but I'm not," I declare randomly.

"Aren't you a virgin?" Chester shrieks.

I blench and hit him violently on the shoulder, cheeks red. He has mastered the art of embarrassing me and I can feel his satisfaction.

"You don't need to know that. That only concerns me," I reply and sip more of my drink so that the alcohol holds me from kicking Chester.

"And Shawn," he adds, and I almost choke on my drink.

He looks at me innocently. I can't help but just smile at him as I shake my head.

"You're such a waste of oxygen," I tease him, and he smirks.

"So are you," he replies immaturely and I giggle.

I wish I had a brother like Chester. My mother is working tonight but my father is at home, giving sweets out to the children.

When I raise my head, I notice that Shawn is staring at me with bright eyes and I can't help but look down at my food. He will drive me crazy. I drink more than I eat. I am pretty sure that I have drunk far too much because the place is already spinning around me. I am feeling too hot, like I could remove all my clothes right now.

"So, who wants to dance?" I suddenly ask in a high-pitched voice after dinner and once again they all look surprised.

"I love you tonight, Ang'," Chester rhapsodizes and stands up but almost falls over because of the quantity of alcohol he has drunk. Shawn is not drinking, nor Kate so they can drive us safely home.

"Scooby be careful', I tell him and we all laugh.

When I stand, I also stumble and almost fall but Tom catches me and I chuckle.

"I was going to feel like Scooby. I mean fall. Yeah, fall, fell, fallen," I sing with an amused voice before chuckling. I should stop drinking.

We finally join in on the dance floor to the rhythm of some really good music. Chester, Shawn and I start dancing like crazy people, throwing our legs, arms and body anywhere we can and laughing. I take a pause to catch my breath and lean against the counter to watch them, well to watch Shawn. Chester and he are performing a kind of choreography to a 90s song. Tom is not far from me; his eyes are glued to Kate.

"You like her, don't you?" I say with a wink and he smiles, uncomfortable. I look at Kate who is smiling and dancing with her sister. "You should. She is great and so are you. You should be together and kiss across the street... yeah, this would be so romantic...Or you should just kiss her now," I say, slurring my words hardly managing to stand straight.

"She can't like me. I'm mute," he says to me in sign language and I feel sorry for him. I wave my hand in front of his face and sigh noisily.

"That's not a reason. You're wonderful and that shit is nothing but a detail. She won't care. I caught her staring at you once."

Thinking that he can't be loved because of his disability is not right. He gives me a sad look that says Really? And I nod and just push him towards Kate. She smiles to him and they start dancing. I give thanks to whoever is playing the music because it's a slow dance. They both blush, dancing close together, Kate's head against Tom's chest. It is wonderful and lovely and romantic.

"Fifa c'mon," Chester calls to me but Shawn walks quickly to me.

"Sorry I have a…" I stop before adding in French, "*Un cavalier.*" Shawn looks playfully at me with a smile at the corner of his lips and I roll my eyes.

"Tom and Kate like each other," I whisper to him during the dance.

"Really? How do you know that?" he asks, surprised.

"I observe better than you, dude," I tease him and we laugh.

But how couldn't he notice that? It's so obvious. I dance with Shawn, forgetting anything else, enjoying him.

"Do you know we can say Moooooooo-jito?" I say the "jito" really quickly. "Moooooooo-jito." I chuckle, finding my joke too funny. "Shawn?" I say in a low voice after a silent pause.

"Fifa." God! Kill me! The way he says it is deep and sensual.

"You smell like Mooooooo-jito," I say as I giggle. Shawn pulls me closer to him and smiles.

"I'm not sure that alcohol is good for you," he states in an amused voice.

"You are good for me," I whisper before noticing it. I want to kick myself but I can't because I am drunk. *What is the link?* My consciousness asks me, sighing like it is tired of me.

"So are you for me," he whispers in my ear and shivers run through my whole body.

I tighten my arms around his neck and he puts his head on the top of mine. I am definitely falling in love with him. This is by far my best Halloween. Everything looks better when we are with the right person.

CHAPTER EIGHTEEN

I am sitting in the passenger seat, staring at Shawn. He is so sexy when he drives. I chuckle at my weird thoughts. He glances at me before focusing again on the road.

"Why do you always chuckle? Do you talk to yourself, like in your head?" he asks in a teasing way.

"I'm the best talker-to-herself," I lazily reply, making him smile. After a few minutes of silence, I say, "Um, Shawn, what are you doing tomorrow?"

"Are you talking to Shawn Shawn or Shawn Mendes?"

I giggle in a very weird way; the alcohol is still playing in my blood. "To Shawn you. Like, Shawn Davis. You don't even look like a Davis. Isn't Davis a British name?" I notice, suddenly serious.

"It's my name anyway. What do I care? Still, it's class," he replies wiggling his eyebrows. I roll my eyes but a small grin is on my face. "Tomorrow, since we don't have class because of the holidays, I'm spending the morning at work."

I hum and straighten up. "Do you ever go to the cemetery to see your family?" I ask him but mentally slap myself for putting it like that. How can I ask someone if he visits his family at the cemetery?

"Sure."

"Why… don't you do it tomorrow? It'll be November first and, in my country, it's important to go and greet our dear dead."

"Do you want to come with me?"

I frown, surprised by the invitation. It's a really intimate moment in my opinion and I would feel a little uncomfortable to be there, but also glad that he wants me to share the moment with him. I gently stroke his shoulder.

"Sure. I would love to meet your family," I answer in a soft voice.

"They'll love you," he answers, looking at me. And we fall silent again.

I would have loved to be invited to his place, have dinner with his family, learn about them and Shawn. This situation seems so sad. Shawn looks sad.

"What do you like?" I suddenly ask. "I mean food, music and all. I want to know you better. I just know that your favorite color is blue, like mine."

"Well, I love gospel music even though I'm not really Christian. I like any kind of music that sounds good to me. I love everything that I can eat."

I roll my eyes. "Is that your answer? Me too, I like any kind of food, but I can say that my favorite one is pounded yam. This is one thing I really miss from my country. Like the real yams and ugh... When I get the chance to go to my country, I eat it like it's the last time. You should too, one day."

"Gee, I love any food as long as there is chicken involved," he answers. A smile finds its way to my lips.

"Much better."

He parks on the driveway. I turn to him, a bit uncomfortable. "So... goodnight?"

"Yeah... goodnight," he replies and smiles at me. I could die for his dimples.

I give him my hand; he looks at me, frowning, but finally squeezes it. I quickly get out of the car and wave at him before running to the door. I run to my room; my parents are not back yet. I take a Halloween shower and head to my room. I first sit at the foot of my bed, in front of my mirror. I have the necklace Shawn gave me in my hand. I wear it everywhere, even when I was avoiding him. When I look at it, I simply remember all the great moments I have spent with Shawn. I watch myself in the mirror and smile. I stand up and kneel down, elbows on the bed, then I close my eyes.

"Dear God, I want to thank you. I want to thank you for everything. Thank you for sending all those great people in my life. I know that I don't usually talk to you, but just know that I love you. Thank you. Protect all of them. All those precious people." I wait for some minutes, trying to hear God through the silence. "I know that you love me too and thank you for that."

***

I'm almost done packing Shawn's and my lunch. I made chicken sandwiches with mustard for both of us because we don't like mayo. I put plenty of salad in mine and added some fruit and drinks besides. I know Shawn is already there because he just texted me. He wrote:

Your man is there. By the way, take a look at these pictures.

Shawn works in an orphanage. He sent me some photos of the children who were playing. I always lose my composure when I see them, when I see hope. I look through the pictures, stars in my eyes.

When I enter the living room, I see my mother who is back from the hospital. She'd been there since last night.

She looks really tired. My father is getting ready for a business lunch.

"So, where are you guys going?" he asks me as he puts his tie on.

"Cemetery," I answer calmly.

They look at me, eyes wide, shocked.

"You guys have a date in a cemetery?" my mother asks, lying on the couch and massaging her forehead. I shrug.

"Yeah, I guess. Bye, love you."

They look at each other, puzzled. I smile once they can't see face.

"Enjoy?" my mother says more like a question.

"We will."

Then I leave the house and walk to Shawn's car with a smile. When I get in, I put the hamper on the floor. I lean towards him to kiss him, but I realize what I am doing and quickly sit back in the sit, blushing.

"Hi," I quickly say, praying that he didn't notice what I almost did.

"I'd have been glad if you did it." Shawn notices everything anyway. I roll my eyes but smile at him.

"My parents were confused when they learnt that we're going to a cemetery," I say amused. Okay, I am changing the subject.

"Didn't you tell them why?"

"No. It was funny." I am laughing hard; my parents are so comical.

"And I'm the crazy one?" He raises an eyebrow, amused.

"Ready for a killer date?" I joke and he smiles as he shakes his head.

I know it's hard for Shawn to do this, so I choose to do what he does for me. I try to make him feel comfortable.

When we reach the cemetery, there aren't many people. We walk through the place; my eyes are wandering among the graves. Some seem to have never been visited while some are carefully tended. We will all end in a grave. It is odd to know that one day, we will all die, and leave everything behind us. Odd to know that our lives are so insignificant, whatever we have in this world, we won't take it to heaven... or hell. *Dear God, I wish to go to heaven. But everyone does.*

We finally reach the place where the three graves are. Brad Davis, 1974–2016. Gabrielle T. Davis, 1976–2015. Mia Davis, 2002–2015. Shawn is staring at the graves silently. I gently stroke his arm and he smiles to me. But suddenly, his face falls.

"What's wrong?"

"I forgot the flowers," he says panicked.

"Don't worry. I bought some. They are in the hamper."

I knew that he would be dreading this day and that he might forget something important like flowers. So, I bought some on my way back from the grocery today. The hamper is very big. Shawn had even asked me why I had brought such a big one.

"Thank you so much," he sighs and I smile at him.

"You're welcome."

We spread the blanket on the ground after putting the flowers on the graves.

"Don't be so stressed. They are happy to know that you are still thinking about them. And that you love them and especially that you have become such a wonderful man."

He smiles sadly. "I would have never thought that you'll be the one giving me advice one day."

"Nor me," I agree, putting my head on his shoulder.

"You'll be a great psychologist," he says in a whisper.

"You too," I say.

We stay silent for a while. Shawn's hand is on my thigh, and I am drawing small circles on the back of it.

"Mia loved the Funny Food. Even when she was not hungry, she would cry for us to go there and we always gave in. We went there so many times, it became our second home. She was their best customer. Even at thirteen she climbed on Tipsy's back and he would run round the restaurant." He stops for a minute, as if he were picturing everything in his mind. "When we went there the last time with your family, I could see her everywhere, in everything. I was remembering her smile. She looked so damn happy. How could anyone know what she was going through?"

I kneel down behind him, put my arms around his neck, and my chin on the hollow of his neck. "She looked happy when she was around you," I whisper, blankly. I remember when Shawn asked me if I am sad again once he is not around. I remember how afraid he was of the answer. He lets out a nervous sigh mixed with chuckles.

"But she was planning her death just next to me."

I tighten my hold on him and kiss him on the neck. Shawn is afraid of sadness, afraid to finish like his family. He is not always happy; he just always looks happy.

"You're amazing, Shawn, and they all loved you so much. You're still here today to fight for them. To change people's life."

Silence returns. It's as if Shawn's parents and Mia were here, smiling at us, hugging Shawn and telling him to keep going. It's so devastating to lose your whole family this way. Shawn is the strongest person I know. He made a pact with happiness: never let me be sad. I sit by him again as he keeps telling me about how it was before.

I can't help but wish that one day, he will have good memories with his own family, he will be the father, and maybe I will be the mother. He will teach his children how to be happy and strong and I guess I will teach them that sadness is part of life. "My father loved dancing, but he danced like shit, like you," he says and we laugh.

It's better to keep the good memories in mind than the bad ones. The good ones remind us how life can be sweet and wonderful.

"I don't. I dance like Beyoncé," I say and pout.

He smirks and says, "If I were Beyoncé, I would send you to jail for insulting me this way." We both laugh. "My mother loved writing, like you. Her writing was so deep, the same way yours is. You women have a way of seeing things men can't see."

"It was a good way for me to handle my feelings." I remember each time I wrote, each tear I cried. I remember how relieved I felt after writing down my feelings.

"And Mia, she was as stubborn as you are. She was always teasing me."

"Nice to meet you, Mia. I like you already," I say to Mia's grave and Shawn smiles.

"You're special," he says in a whisper.

"How am I special?"

"I don't know many girls who would accept a date in a cemetery, let alone talk to dead people and talk about them as if they were here. It's so creepy."

"Normal people are boring," I say simply and we laugh.

"We haven't even eaten," Shawn says after pulling out of the parking lot.

"It could have been the creepiest thing ever, because I'm sure that we would have done it as if they were there, eating with us."

"Yeah, I guess. You would have forced me to."

I roll my eyes but smile. We park on a kind of deserted road because cars hardly pass here. From here, the view is wonderful. Shawn helps me to climb on the trunk. "Let me help you, my little pet," he teases me.

We eat, staring at the landscape and talking. We finally fall asleep, my head against his shoulder, leaning against the windshield. Soon, we will have to wake up, he will go to work and I will wait for him to be done. I will wait for him again and again. Shawn deserves that.

CHAPTER NINETEEN

After cleaning up, I stay in the kitchen, drinking hot chocolate and working. My father enters the kitchen and I glance at him with a smile. He gives me the "talk" look. I put my pen down and watch him. He pours some whisky into a glass with ice and sits in front of me. He looks tired; he mostly works at home. And he works too much.

"You know that I'm not really okay with you being a psychologist, don't you?" he asks.

My father has kept the African point of view about jobs like psychology. They don't really see how important it is. I could probably even count the people who have ever been to a psychologist in their life in Benin, on my fingers.

"Yup? I literally begged you to let me do this program," I remind him, biting into a marshmallow.

"Hmm, yes. But I understand how important it is for you. I have that friend, Hank, he has a practice not far away. I asked him if he could take you for an internship."

"Seriously!"

"Yes. I know that you don't want me to interfere with your professional life—"

"No, it's fine, dad. Thank you," I cut him off with a smile.

I am supposed to find an internship to start next year, but it's a great help to have one already lined up. I know that I'll only be able to maybe watch but it's so exciting, but scary.

"So… how was your date?" he asks uncomfortably. I am more talkative with my mother than my father but it's nice that he tries.

"Good."

"Are you back together?"

"No, Dad. We're friends."

He narrows his eyes at me but shrugs. "All right."

***

"So, you've got an internship?" Shawn asks me while driving to the Double A.

"Yes, but not a real, real one. Just a kind of watcher or assistant."

"That's really great. You should enjoy that opportunity."

"Yes, I will. You're lucky that you can do all that you do for orphans. I'm glad to find something for me too."

We finally arrive at the restaurant; the team is there already. There is a big poster with Tom and his parents' pictures that says "Happy Birthday Double A." They organized a party to celebrate the restaurant's birthday. Free food for their best customers. As soon as we enter, I spot Tom and Caroline, hand in hand. Caroline blushes as I wave at them with a smile. Caroline is like those fashion girls always cool and all, she's very different from Tom, but they make a nice couple. We sit at a table.

"Good evening, everyone. Today is Double A's birthday. So, enjoy," Alicio says loudly, his face flushed, with his wife beside him.

They serve their best foods and Italian music is playing. Everyone is eating and talking. Chester is really quiet tonight; this is extremely strange. When I try to tease him by tickling him, he laughs weakly. I suck a strand of spaghetti with as much noise as possible but again he is not very enthusiastic. I glance at Shawn who shrugs but I'm sure he knows much more than I do. Chester is his best friend after all. While everyone is dancing, Chester and Shawn are sitting at a table and talking. I stare at them. Chester runs his hands through his hair nervously; I even spot a tear at the corner of his eye. Shawn seems to be comforting him.

"Hi Fifa." Kate appears suddenly, making me jump.

"Hey," I say uncomfortably, looking at her.

I finally found the difference between the twins. Caroline has a small circular birthmark at the between her collarbones. I glance across the room and spot Tom and Caroline dancing and flirting and kissing. They are cute.

"What do you think about Tom and your sister?" I ask her and she glances at them with a bright smile.

"She has always liked him, even before he got that voice problem. And I am glad to see them finally together." I smile at her answer. I have read that twins are really close and can even feel what each other feels. I was afraid that Tom would be a problem for them. "What do you think they are talking about?" she asks me, gesturing at Shawn and Chester with her chin.

I shrug. "I have no idea."

"I'm sure that slut hurt him again," she says bitterly. I look at her, curious.

"Which slut?"

She frowns and stares at me as if she were trying to work out if I am joking.

"Seriously? You don't know?" I am really confused. "His girlfriend. She's a slut. She keeps cheating on him and hiding their relationship from a lot of people."

My eyes are wide. "Chester has a girlfriend?" I am really surprised to hear that. He doesn't look like a couple's guy. "And why does she never hang out with you guys?" She just gives me a *guess why* look. "She is... ashamed of him?" I ask in a really confused tone.

"She doesn't know how special he is. She just can't understand him," she answers, looking sadly at Chester. I would have never imagined all what is dawning on me right now. Chester has a girlfriend. As Chester is Chester, and so special, she can't bear it. By seeing the way, he is affected, he loves her. But the worse is that...

"You like him?" I almost scream, she looks down and blushes. "Oh my God! You guys would be the final couple of the group. Why don't you tell him?"

"He loves her, really. You should see how happy he looked when she cared for him. It has been two years, two long years that she's been a slut, but Chester keeps hoping. She wanted Shawn first and as she couldn't get him..."

An acid bile burns in my throat when I hear that. If I were starting to hate that girl for hurting Chester, I hate her even more for hurting Chester to get back at Shawn.

"She used to hang out with us just to see Shawn. But since she heard that he has a girlfriend, she has stopped. Chester and Shawn are so blind. Chester because he doesn't notice how much of a slut she is and both of them to not be able to notice how fond of Shawn she is."

I let out a cold breath to take in all that Kate is telling me. My eyes land on Shawn. I realize how I can't lose him, how many other girls may want him and somehow, I just want him to be mine... only mine. My chest hurts at the thought that someone could take him from me. I finally walk over to them; they stop talking as soon as I sit. I try to hide my discomfort, to just smile at them.

"What are you talking about?" I try to ask. They look at each other and then back at me.

"About... hair?" Shawn states with an unsure voice and Chester rolls his eyes.

I don't know if I should bring up the subject of his girlfriend right now or just wait. Somehow, it hurts me that he doesn't even think of telling me about something like that. I know we just met two months ago. But I thought we had a real friendship, or maybe it's just because he is Shawn's best friend.

"What are you thinking about?" Shawn suddenly asks me.

"Hair?" I reply, annoyed.

***

"Now, tell me. What's wrong?" We are in front of my house. Shawn turns to me, an arm on the steering wheel.

"You tell me," I reply and he rolls his eyes. I turn to him and bite my lips while staring at his. I lean in to kiss him, but he backs away, taken aback.

"What are you doing?" he asks uncomfortably but I don't answer. "I thought you wanted to go slow. Friend first?"

I kiss him on the lips but he doesn't kiss me back, this is frustrating me.

"Do you know about Chester's girlfriend?" I ask as he frowns.

"What does she have to do with the fact that you're trying to kiss me right now? Wait, Kate put those creepy ideas in your head, didn't she?"

I don't respond. I lean in again to kiss him, but he gently pushes me back.

"Just shut up and kiss me," I whine but once again he pushes me away.

I sit back in my seat and sigh noisily. I nervously run my hand through my hair.

"Why don't you want to kiss me? You like her?" I snap with anger.

Shawn looks annoyed. "God, Fifa you tried to kiss me just because you thought I might like her? And who says she does like me? She is Chester's girlfriend."

"But also, a slut," I say even though I don't know her. But only a bad person would hurt Chester the way she seems to.

"You don't even know her," Shawn says.

"Because you do?" I ask with a challenging look.

He sighs. "I don't even want to talk about this. You're the one who wanted us to be friends first. You tried to kiss me just because you didn't like the idea of me with someone else. I rejected you because I don't want things to be like that between us. Then you're angry?" Shawn shouts, making me feel guilty. "You know that you're the only one on my mind. You do know how crazy I am about you. She doesn't like me and even if she does? Who cares? I don't give a shit about her and Chester should also stop thinking about that toxic girl who's messing with his heart."

I stay silent. I hurt Shawn with what I had tried to do. I tried to use him because I want him to be mine. I am the one who brought up the friendship thing, but I was the one trying to break it with bad thoughts.

"Sorry," I whisper.

Shawn runs his hand through his hair.

"It's nothing. Just trust me sometimes," he sighs and I nod. "Come here," he says, and I climb in his lap to hug him. My head is in the hollow of his neck and he is gently walking his fingers over my back. "I would never do that to you."

"I know."

I kiss him on the cheek and get out of the car. But somehow, I know that I will hate that girl. I know that Shawn has not told me everything to not scare me. And then again, I am afraid. But this time, to lose him. But most of all, afraid for Chester and Shawn; of what that girl could do to their friendship.

CHAPTER TWENTY

W e are all hanging out tonight at Chester's, the house where I met them for the first time. He has got through his bad mood of yesterday. At least he looks better right now, pulling Kate's hair and teasing her. They look cute together. People just don't realize how their behavior can impact deeply on someone else's life. That girl, Chester's girlfriend, she doesn't know how much she is hurting him, or maybe she does but just doesn't care. Shawn sits by me, wraps his arm round my shoulder and leans back against the couch. I am staring at Chester and Kate. She does like him, the way he is. But he doesn't even notice that someone so close to him is fond of him, because he is being hurt by someone else. Shawn slowly brings his mouth closer to my ear and I feel a shiver run through my body.

But suddenly something cold touches my ear, making me jump. "Shawn!" I scream as I stand up from the couch.

He spits the ice into his cup, chuckles and pulls me onto him. After falling onto him, I quickly move to sit by him.

"It's crazy that he doesn't know that she loves him, isn't it?" Shawn whispers in my ear.

I take a look at Kate and Chester. They are so deep in conversation that they don't even notice us. Liam is concentrating on his phone while Tom and Caroline are focused on each other in the kitchen.

"Give me a couple of minutes," I say to Shawn and stand up. "Chester, come here," I call to him, already walking out to his garden. Before I turn around, Kate gives me a *What are you going to tell him?* look.

When we sit in the garden, I adjust the jacket around myself. "Chester, why didn't you tell me that you have a girlfriend?" I ask, looking into his eyes to catch any clue.

He stays silent for a while before speaking. "I guess, I didn't want you to pity me or see me differently," he answers while looking away.

"Because she's behaving badly to you?"

"Because I'm letting her do it," he corrects me through a whisper.

"Do you love her?" I dare to ask, even though the answer is clear.

"What do you think?" he groans.

Still, I am not sure that he loves her the way he is supposed to. Like when I see him with Kate, he seems so happy that I would bet that he has feelings for her. We both stare at the sky for a while before I speak.

"You know, Chester, I know that you've heard so much 'If she does that, she doesn't deserve you,' or 'You don't have to change for anyone.' But those two statements are true. I know you better, Chester, I know it's hard to handle feelings and all, but God gave us that power. If we don't try, we may never know what we can do and how strong we can be." I turn to him and gently squeeze his shoulder. "I know you well enough to say that she's not good for you. All that you have to know is that you're the one supposed to stop this suffering for yourself, for your heart," I say in a friendly tone and he smiles at me. It feels weird to have a serious conversation with him. "You could try dating other girls, for instance," I add casually.

"You mean Kate?" As soon as he says it, I frown, taken aback. "You all think that I'm dumb or crazy, but I have feelings. I just don't like being serious all the time because it's painful actually. That's why I just go around making jokes. It's better."

"Like Shawn," I whisper for me.

"Yeah. But he got the chance to fall for you. I just got the bad luck to love someone like Hannah."

"I understand," I simply reply, blankly.

"You're a good friend Fifa. Shawn should never let you go because you're a great person. He is happy with you."

I smile to him as he squeezes my hands. After a while, we walk back to the living room.

"Seriously Chester, you don't want to steal Fifa from Shawn by any chance, do you?" Liam welcomes us back and I roll my eyes.

"I'm right here Liam," I warn him; he smirks.

"I know."

I go to find a drink in the kitchen and walk back to the living room. The doorbell rings so I open the door on my way back. It's a brown-haired girl with amazing purple eyes. She is beautiful with her short hair and her slim face.

"Hello," I say.

"Hi. I'm Hannah. Is Chester around?" I almost choke on my drink. She has a high-pitched, slightly arrogant voice. She is dressed casually but the bright green of her clothes, seems flashy and over the top. Her makeup is overdone.

"Hannah? You're Hannah?" I ask again.

She rolls her eyes and enters without answering.

"Hi guys," she says once in the living room.

Everyone freezes. I choose to keep a low profile. Chester stands up and walks over to her.

"What are you doing here?" he asks nervously.

"Well, my boyfriend texted me yesterday and said that he wanted us to talk," she starts sarcastically. "So, here I am to talk."

Kate is glaring at her. No one seems to like her here.

"That was yesterday, and you didn't bother to reply," he answers coldly.

He's trying to be patient. We should leave to give them some privacy, but we are paralyzed and just too curious.

"Stop being so dramatic, Chester," she grouses as she rolls her eyes.

"I think you should leave, Hannah," Shawn intervenes standing up.

She glares at him but smiles. "Shawn is far a better kisser than you. The best I've ever had," she simpers.

Everyone's mouths fall open. Shawn's blood seems to drain from his face; he's frozen to the spot. My heart opens the door to leave this place, but my body is not moving. Shawn and Hannah? Hannah and Shawn? Chester's best friend and Chester's girlfriend? My ex-boyfriend, current friend-flirt with Chester's girlfriend?

"Stop saying shit and just leave," Chester barks and pulls her towards the door but she violently pushes him back.

"Don't touch me, asshole!" she screams. "You know what? I'm glad that this thing is done. You were bothering me. I never loved you, Chester. I never even cared for you. All this time I wanted Shawn. Not you. And guess what? I had him."

I suck in a breath, my legs shaking. I would have said that she's lying but Shawn's face right now is telling the opposite.

"Tell him the truth Shawn," she screams louder. "Tell him we kissed."

Chester turns to Shawn but as soon as he notices his look, he backs away. "No..." he whispers, shaking his head. He runs his tongue over his lips, blinks several times. His cheeks are red as he clenches his fists.

"Chester. I swear that she's twisting the truth," Shawn tries to explain and I feel tears falling on my cheeks. Shawn would do that? He wouldn't. It doesn't make sense.

"You and me, we're done," Chester hisses to Hannah.

She claps her hands together. "Thank God," she snaps. She turns on her heel and stops by me. She looks down at me and chuckles before leaving.

"I'm not letting this happen," Shawn groans as he runs out of the house. No one moves.

Shawn comes back a short time later holding Hannah by the arm; she's struggling and telling him to let go of her.

"Tell them the truth, now," Shawn shouts at her.

"Okay," she sighs. He releases her, and she adjusts her outfit before talking.

"I met Shawn before you and this whole story. We met in a coffee shop and I kissed him. Well, I tried, and he rejected me. We didn't go farther because he's stupidly uptight. He told me when I met you to not tell you about it."

"You're just a bitch," Chester starts. "Just leave," he adds calmly. "Leave!" he orders louder, making all of us jump. She walks out quickly.

"And you..." he hisses, pointing at Shawn before leaving the room.

This is so much information to assimilate. Chester runs to his room and I'm sure that he is going to cry.

"Fifa," Shawn begs walking toward me.

"I trust you," I whisper even though this is hurting me.

I am somehow relieved that he hadn't done that. It would have broken my heart and destroyed my opinion of Shawn. I smile to him, then hug him. Kate takes big steps towards Chester's room.

"I think we should leave; you'll talk to him later. Just not now," I tell him gently and he nods.

The drive home is very quiet.

"Thanks for trusting me."

"It's nothing. I was scared when she threw that bomb at first. But I understand what you did for Chester."

"I thought that I was doing the right thing. Chester was so deep into her and in love. I didn't want him to fall from that cloud. I thought she just had a small crush on me and that she'd end up falling for him. But she never did."

"He'll forgive you. You guys are best friends and you respected him."

Shawn sighs loudly but smiles. "He's more than that, he is like a brother. But he is so obsessed with that girl that I don't know if he'll be able to forgive me for her loving me."

"He will. One, because this is not your fault, and two, because it is a true friendship." I kiss Shawn on the forehead and smile at him.

Once in my room, I let out a deep sigh. I lie down on the floor to cry. I need to; I just need to let all this out. I was right about her. I don't even know how to feel. I know that Shawn is innocent, but I can't free myself from the pain eating my heart. I kneel down, the same way I've been doing every night for some days and pray. *Dear God, please fix the situation between Shawn and Chester. Amen.*

CHAPTER TWENTY-ONE

*H*appiness tip ten: Don't keep any trouble for too long on your mind.

I send the text to Shawn, chewing on my bottom lip. I know that he is sad about Chester not talking to him any more. I get out of bed to get ready for class. It's still early so I can get the time to talk with Shawn and maybe to Chester. I wear a cream skirt with a grey sweater and head to the kitchen after tying my hair in a bun, as usual. I greet Mother and Dad a wet kiss on each cheek.

"Morning!" I say to them.

"Good morning, princess," they both reply.

I still don't feel at all like a nineteen-year-old girl but more like I'm still in high school, yet I don't really care. I grab an apple, wash it, and sit to read my notes.

"Hank said that you should meet him on Wednesday about your internship," my father tells me while reading his newspaper.

My stomach turns at the thought that I will be around so many people who, unlike me, chose to talk, talk to make things better in their lives.

"All right, I'll make sure I'm ready."

After parking my car, I spot Shawn taking something from his. I quietly run to him. I jump on him and shout boo. He starts but turns to me with a smile that I return. "Hello, Mr Davis."

"Hi Miss Lawson, soon-to-be Mrs Davis," he replies as he puts his hands on my hip to pull me closer to him. I give him a light kiss on the lips. "I thought we were just friends," he teases me and I quickly back away, blushing.

How can I always forget that rule that I set myself? "I don't know why I always forget that," I whine. "Let's start over again." He smirks, amused.

"You are impossible," he observes, shaking his head.

I give him my hand; he stares at it for a few seconds before squeezing it, still amused but puzzled.

"Good morning, my friend," I start over in a very formal tone. At least I hope that it is, because his hand is very warm despite the cold. It makes me melt.

"Hello, Miss Lawson, soon-to-be Mrs Davis," he repeats playfully. I hit him on the shoulder.

"You're not supposed to say that," I remind him.

He takes his bag from the car and closes the door. As we are walking together, he replies, "I'm supposed to say that."

When we reach the entrance of our faculty, I spot Chester walking toward his. As soon as he sees us, his face drops and he looks away abruptly. This is much more serious than I thought it was. He looks tired though. Worse, he is dressed very casually for once, in all black. Shawn tenses and his jaw tightens. I have two options: quickly walk with Shawn to class or act like Chester. I look around and inhale deeply to give myself some courage.

"Chester!" I shout. His eyes go wide, clearly surprised by my guts; he looks away. Shawn doesn't say anything. No one would ever think that I would dare to do this and honestly, nor would I. "Chester! He ho!" I shout louder, waving at Chester. I glue my eyes on him to block out everyone's stare. I walk down the stairs to run to him. "Chester!" I stop in front of him. He takes a step to the left of me, but I climb on his back. Shawn's eyes go wide. *Yeah, I am a little bit crazy.*

"You're crazy, Fifa, get down," Chester exclaims but I can hear his amusement.

"No, I want you to drive me to my class, CC. And in case you don't understand, CC means Cab Chester," I protest.

He leans back to force me to climb off of him, but I resist. He finally gives up.

"You're a big baby," he sighs. "And you're too heavy," he complains, and I smack him on the head. "Ouch," he groans like a bear.

"Say that I'm heavy again and I'll smack you harder," I threaten, praying that no member of the administration sees us.

"You're a whale," he continues and I smack him again, making him chuckle. When we join Shawn, they look away from each other. I have to find a solution. It's an emergency.

"Shawn, what do you think about a normal Chester? Did you even know that he had normal clothes in his closet?" At least Chester and Shawn are walking together. Being on Chester's back is comfortable, I could get used to it. Shawn glances at him.

"Nice."

"Do you guys remember when you first met? You said that it was the magic meeting of the forever friendship, remember?" No one answers me and we are already in front of the classroom. I sigh and climb off Chester. "Thank you."

"Welcome," he says, already walking toward his faculty. I gently squeeze Shawn's shoulder.

"Everything will be fine," I whisper to him before kissing him on the cheek.

The day flies by and there is no Chester around. He just broke up with his girlfriend and has lost his best friend. That sucks. I text Kate to tell her to look after him. She replies that tomorrow is Chester's birthday. That gives me an idea. I hope that it will work. Fortunately, I just have one class tomorrow since there is some sort of lecturers' meeting.

***

"I made Chester's favorite cake" I announce, walking into the living room.

The whole team is there except Kate, who is supposed to bring Chester, and Chester himself. Shawn has just arrived, right after work. Chester has been avoiding me like the plague because he knows that I will never agree with this useless conflict between Shawn and him. I decided to play one last card even though I'm not sure that he will come. But Kate assured me that she knows how to convince him, and I trust her. We have a huge terrace behind the house, giving onto the garden. We decorated it and made a big poster: Happy birthday Chester aka Cab Chester aka Scooby-Doo aka Food Man. We kind of rushed since we didn't have much time to prepare it. Tom's parents made different kinds of pizza: margherita, *napoletana, regina* and one that I forget the name of. They look really tasty. For sure, Chester will love them.

I made a cream cake mixed with a chocolate cake. Chester likes any cake with at least two different flavors. Chester loves chocolate and Shawn is fond of vanilla cream, so I mixed their tastes. We made some fruit juices and *bissap* because I don't really like soda. I took one of the best champagnes that my father has. Shawn had been staring at me since his arrival before walking out to the terrace. When I join him, he is sitting on one of the outside chairs, staring into distance.

"What if he doesn't even come?" He breaks the silence with an insecure voice that breaks my heart.

"He will," I whisper and wrap my arms around his waist.

He squeezes my hand and I smile against his neck.

"You clearly don't know what a friendship is," he observes playfully, referring to the way I always behave like his girlfriend. I just can't help it. I walk to stay in front of him.

"At least I know that Cab Chester and you have a real one. You and I can create our own type," I answer seductively, walking my fingers on his collarbone. He rolls his eyes but smiles. The way he is staring at me right now could make me melt. "What?" I ask, suddenly feeling shy.

He pulls me closer to him and wraps his arms round my waist. His head is in the hollow of my neck as his wet lips are against my skin. I am almost shaking with what I'm feeling in my body.

"We are not meant to be friends," he moans against me, making me chuckle nervously. I detach myself from him but he doesn't remove his arms.

"We are," I object.

He pulls me back to him, then presses his lips to mine. I don't even want to resist, so I kiss him back. Our lips are enjoying coming back together; I am delighted to feel his soft and smart mouth against mine. I wrap my arms around his neck and pull his head closer to mine.

He smiles against my lips. When we stop kissing, I try to catch my breath, staring at his lips. I press my forehead to his and our breaths mix, slowly, lovely. "We aren't," he whispers again, making me smile.

Someone clearing their throat, pushes me to back away abruptly, my heart racing. My parents are not around; my mother is at the hospital and my father is at the office, but you never know. Besides, I really don't want my mother to catch me again in this kind of position or my father to even ever see this. He likes Shawn, but I am not sure that he will appreciate catching him cuddling and kissing his daughter. I exhale loudly when I notice that it's just Liam.

"Um, Chester is here," he declares with a grin somewhere between uncomfortable and teasing that says *You guys are funny.*

I run my hands through my hair and smile to Liam. "Thank you, we're coming."

I look at Shawn and notice that he is less stressed. I take his hand and we walk back to the living room. Chester is not sitting; he is standing near the lobby, staring at Shawn's and my intertwined hands.

"Back together?" he asks harshly.

I quickly nod. I don't really know if Shawn and I are back together, but at least I know that kiss meant many things. That I need him, he needs me and that we are not meant to be friends. I walk over to Chester, but Shawn doesn't move while smiling to him.

"I'm glad that you're here. Happy birthday." I can see that Chester wants to treat me the same way he is treating Shawn, but he just can't, because he sees all the effort that I'm making to ease this situation.

"Thank you for all this," he says. I glance at Kate who is smiling uncomfortably.

"Let's party then," Liam shouts in a very funny voice that brings the tension down.

"Yeah," I agree, thankful to Liam. "Help me to bring the stuff to the terrace," I add.

We stay on the terrace despite the cold. Chester doesn't really eat, neither does Shawn. As I'm really hungry from everything that's happened, I choose to just listen to my stomach for once. I eat for the two of them but promise myself secretly that they will eat the cake at least. Everyone is talking and joking except our two best friends.

"Yeah, Chester shits in their garden because they never clean their bathroom," Liam giggles and everyone burst out laughing, even Chester.

"Oh my God! You're so crazy and disgusting Cab Chester," I tease him. He sticks his tongue out at me and I chuckle.

"That was not my fault. I have been going to that house for so long and they never cleaned their bathroom. At least since that they started to, to avoid people doing what I did," he says proudly, and I shake my head. His eyes meet Shawn's, but he quickly looks away. *They are so childish.*

"Let's play truth or dare," Caroline suggests when everyone stops talking.

"Sounds good," Kate replies.

"So, Shawn, truth or dare?" Liam starts.

"Truth."

"How far have you and Fifa been?" he asks. I blush at his indiscreet question.

"What sort of question is that? Are you crazy? What business do you guys have in my privacy?" I snap uncomfortably, but all of them seem to be waiting for Shawn's answer.

"Well..." I bury my head in my hands because I am so embarrassed. "Kiss, cuddle and some other stuff," Shawn says cooly.

"What other stuff?" Caroline asks playfully.

"His turn is passed. He has answered," I point out.

"What are you so afraid of?" Liam insists slyly, making me roll my eyes.

I don't even know why I am being this shy, when Shawn and I have never gone far. I don't even know how to tell them that I want to stay a virgin till my wedding, or at least that I want to be completely sure of my love before having sex. Clearly Shawn and I don't know each other enough to have reached that stage.

"Kate, truth or dare?" Shawn asks her.

"Dare," she chooses proudly.

Shawn smirks. "French kiss Liam."

Everyone's eyes go wide, even Kate's. What is Shawn doing? I follow his gaze that is on Chester. Chester has clenched his fists, seeming angry. Does this mean that he isn't that indifferent to Kate? Kate slowly stands up and starts walking to Liam.

"I mean Chester. Kiss Chester," Shawn corrects himself in a really calm tone, staring confidently at Chester.

Kate sighs in relief before turning on Chester. She is suddenly shy, which she is not usually. She leans in to kiss Chester. They kiss slowly in the beginning and then Kate's hands slip into Chester's hair and Chester puts his hands on her hips. They actually kiss for a while; we watch them as if it was a spectacle.

"I will die single," Liam groans before leaning against the bench.

His interruption makes all of us laugh. His remark seems to bring Chester and Kate back to our world. Kate sits, blushing. When her eyes land on me, I give her a smile.

"Fif, truth or dare?" she asks.

"Truth."

"Who is funnier between Shawn and Chester?"

Why is she asking me that question? I don't want to answer any question that concerns Shawn and Chester. I clear my throat, embarrassed. I glance at her and she gives me an *oops* look. "Well... they are both funny and very different in their jokes, but I'll admit that Chester is a funnier character," I answer honestly, chewing on my bottom lip.

"Yeah. How can someone who steals his best friend's girl be funny anyway?" Chester replies coldly. I just want to bury myself because this is not going to end well.

"I never stole her. I don't even care about her," Shawn answers impatiently.

"That's not what I understood. Maybe you're actually fucking her while lying to Fif," Chester continues, making my chest hurt.

Shawn stands up and clenches his fists, Chester does also.

"Respect her," Shawn threatens, jaw contracted. I know that Chester is angry but he doesn't have the right to speak like that. What he said hurt me.

"You, do you respect her? Did you respect me? You're a real dick, Shawn." Chester doesn't give up, spitting venom.

"You know what? I don't even want to be friend with a wimp any more. Fuck you," Shawn replies harshly, clearly annoyed. We are all watching, afraid to intervene.

"Okay, I just hope that your parents are not disappointed with what you've become. Mia would be," Chester barks.

"Chester, you're going too far," I warn him.

"I guess, your parents were relieved to leave you to live here alone because seriously, Chester, you're just..."

"Stop!" I shout, feeling my vocal cords vibrate. I know that they don't believe a word of what they're saying. I don't want them to say things they will regret all their lives. We should never let our anger speak for us. I'm appalled by their behavior. I walk to Chester and slap him and then do the same with Shawn. Everyone is staring at me with wide eyes. "We set all this up to fix things between you, but since you guys want to act like children, maybe it's all right," I bluster while clapping my hands together. "No, it's not," I sigh and start to walk away to the living room. "Chester, now," I say firmly, and he follows me. I am sure that he glares at Shawn.

I stand in the living room, arms crossed. "Sit down," I order in a bossy tone. He obeys. "What's wrong?" I ask him softly, looking at him.

He runs his hand through his hair and sighs. "I'm acting like a dick, I know."

I sit next to him. "So, why are you acting like this? You know that Shawn would never do that, don't you?"

"Yes, I just... I'm just so pissed off that I had to be angry with everyone but myself," he confesses.

I gently put my hand on his shoulder and squeeze it. "That girl is the only culprit here. Neither you nor Shawn. Just her."

"Yeah, I know. Sorry for all this," he sighs and I smile at him.

"It's all right."

"I never did that and I never would. You're my brother and I could have never done that even if I wanted to, which was not the case." We both lift our heads up to look at Shawn, who is standing in the doorway; Chester stands up. They are like two lovers who are trying to solve their problems. It's cute and a bit scary.

"I'm sorry, bro... Your parents are surely proud of you. I love you brother," Chester says and they hug each other. I have tears in my eyes.

"Shawn, I'm breaking up with you because you're cheating on me right in front of me," I joke and we burst into laughter.

"We'd make a better couple anyway," Chester replies, making both Shawn and I roll our eyes. Chester is definitely the brother I never got the chance to have.

"Any sane girl would be happy to have you as boyfriend," Shawn tells him, patting his shoulder.

"I guess that I should start looking for that sane girl," Chester says, as he gives *the look* to Kate who is standing by the door. Oh my God!

"Happy birthday to you," we sing to Chester. We are all standing around the cake.

"Make a wish," I tell him.

"I wish to always be faithful to all the people who love me," he wishes. This is cute and he particularly looks at Kate. She has been such a great support for him through this situation. "I'm joking. I wish I always eat Fif's cake for the rest of my life and also Kate's delicious meat pies," he corrects himself and we all laugh.

We eat the cake in front of some Netflix shows. Chester spreads cake on Kate's nose and she hits him on the shoulder. He smirks and kisses her on the cheek, then she blushes. Aw, cutie.

"Thank you," Shawn whispers to me. My head is against his shoulder as we sit on the floor and lean against the couch.

"By the way, Fif, are we going to talk about the fact that you slapped us?" Chester remarks loudly; I giggle.

"I confess that it was a secret dream of mine," I reply playfully, and everyone laughs.

I do love this chapter of my life, I love these new characters who suddenly entered in and made it nicer, greater and lovely.

CHAPTER TWENTY-TWO

I've just come back from school, I rush into the shower. After, I spend at least thirty minutes in front of my dresser trying to find something presentable to wear. This internship is stressing me out. I have to be perfect. First, because it will allow me to know if I am able to handle the job. Second, if I do well, Dr Hank Johns will maybe take me on for official internships or even employ me after my degree. I finally decide to wear grey pencil pants, a white top, black blazer and wedge shoes to make me look less short. I look at myself in the mirror and like what I see. I blink and strike some silly, seductive poses to forget how stressed I am. I drive to his office; the drive is shorter than I thought. Still, the office is out of town. As I close the door of the car, I take a deep breath before walking toward the building.

"Good morning Dr Johns, I'm really glad to be here with you," I say to myself, walking blindly. "Come on, Fifa, it's not a date," I remind to myself, groaning. "Good morning…"

I suddenly bump into someone. When I raise my eyes, they fall on a forty-year-old man with broad shoulders and blond hair, wearing glasses. He seems to take care of himself. "I'm so sorry," I start to apologize nervously.

"Don't worry," he cuts me off with a warm smile.

I give him an awkward smile before striding towards the office. I don't want to be late. The man surely felt my stress, especially because I was talking to myself.

When I enter, I walk towards the secretary. It's a nice young lady with blue eyes and short hair tinted in grey. She smiles at me.

"Good morning, I'm Fifame Lawson," I tell her.

"Oh, hello Miss Lawson. Dr Johns went to deal with something. He will be right back," she answers. "You can sit over there." She points at a seat.

"Thank you."

I walk to the corner of the lobby where there are a couple of couches. I sit and wait, looking around and tapping my knees with my fingers. So, this is what a psychologist office looks like. The place is very well kept, with some flowers in vases; the couches are comfortable and the wallpaper is simple and relaxing. I spot the secretary looking at me; she gives me smile. I clumsily look away after smiling back at her. I am sure she's wondering how I think I can plan to be a psychologist while I act like a patient. I didn't even ask her name. I stand up uncomfortably and walk over to her with a nervous smile.

"Can I help you?" she asks nicely. I clear my throat; my hands are laid flat on the counter.

"Um... I was wondering your name," I stammer and she giggles. What is so funny? Am I funny? In a good or bad way?

"I'm Stacy Brown, from Florida," she answers.

"Oh great! I love Florida even though I've never been there," I continue, more and more stressed. "So, I'm going to sit back down," I quickly add and walk back to the couch. I see her shaking her head and smiling. I don't know if she is making fun of me or if she likes me.

The door flies open, a sixteen — or seventeen — year old blond boy enters. He has a neutral expression on his face when he quickly talks with the lady. After quiet exchange, he sits next to me. His features are Asian, I would say Korean, but his complexion is brown. This is a weird mix, but I like it. He is actually kind of handsome.

"Hello, do you have an appointment with Dr Johns?" I ask him kindly, but he glares at me. All right, nice. He turns his head to look at an invisible point. *Fif, come on, he's here for a reason. Give him another chance. Your work will be to make people talk to you.* A scar crosses his right eye from the eyelid to the top of his cheeks.

"I love your scar," I say quietly. Oh my God, I am insane. *How can I like a scar? What if something terrible happened to him and caused that?*

When he says "thank you" in a nice voice, I reassure myself that it may work. After a few seconds of silence, he turns to me.

"Do you really like it or are you saying that just to be nice or to make fun of me?" he asks with narrowed eyes, as if he wanted to read on my face whether I am lying or not.

"I really like it, it's cool. Um, you look like those guys in the movies who look bad but are actually the sweetest people," I answer honestly. The corners of his lips turn up, and he smiles to me.

"I like your face too," he replies casually.

"I know, I'm gorgeous," I simper as I sweep my hair up like Ludmila from Violetta. He chuckles, rolling his eyes. "What are you doing here?" I ask him; his smile fades. "Oh, I'm sorry. That is between you and Dr Johns, sorry." I quickly correct myself.

"I'm here to talk," he answers quietly with a hint of sadness in his eyes.

"That is a good thing," I assure him, a small smile on my lips. I respect anyone able to let out his feelings, able to talk. Because, never have I been that strong.

"What about you?"

"I've an internship."

My phones beeps and I see that it's a text from Shawn. *How is it going so far? Stay calm and relax. Kiss you.*

He is so nice. When I start to reply, the boy by me speaks up reading the text without any discretion, "Your boyfriend?"

"Yeah," I answer with a smile.

At the same time, the man I bumped into earlier enters the room. He smiles to Stacy before walking over to us.

"Good morning, Miss Lawson, I'm very glad to see you," he says to me as he shakes my hand. Oh my God! I just want to die. I bumped into my boss.

"Good morning Dr Johns," I start, chewing on my bottom lip. "I'm really sorry for earlier. I..."

"Don't worry, it's fine. I knew it was you. And between you and me, I was also distracted," he answers. There is something in his voice that inspires peace and confidence. He was born for this job, unlike people like me.

"Hassan, you finally decided to come. We'll start now, follow me."

Hassan stands up. "I want her to be with us." I am wide-eyed when he says it.

"Me?" I repeat. "I... don't think this is a good idea. I'm not a professional."

"Actually, I'm not allowed to let you speak to someone who isn't a professional, but my job is to make you comfortable. So, Fifame can come," Dr Johns says, and I feel my heart beating too fast.

When we reach the room, Hassan sits on a big couch, clearly stressed, while Dr Johns sits in a much smaller one. I walk to the one next to window and sit uncomfortably. I breathe with difficulty. I have avoided psychologist's offices all my life, but here I am for the first time in the role of a future psychologist.

"Good morning, Hassan, how are you feeling?" Dr Johns starts nicely.

Hassan glances at me, as if he wanted to find reassurance in me. I smile at him. I feel like my presence here helps him, and that warms my heart. I try as much as I can to hide my discomfort, to give him confidence. "Fine. I'm fine."

"All right. Tell me everything. Sit as comfortably as you can, close your eyes and take a deep breath. No one is here. Talk to yourself. Say all that is paining you and all that is annoying you and weighing on your heart."

Hassan sits more comfortably, shoeless. He lets his head fall back and breathes deeply. "I... I've been thinking about coming here for two months," he starts quietly.

"And why didn't you?" Dr Johns asks him.

"I was afraid. I think that I was more afraid of letting it all out than keeping it inside." His voice is shaky, really different from the cold one of earlier.

I think he just wanted to build a barrier to not let me hurt him; I am sure people have hurt him. I feel it. Everyone gets hurt. There isn't a human being who has never hurt or been hurt. "And why did you show up today?" Dr Johns looks extremely calm.

"Because it's too much for me to handle. Besides, you're a stranger and I will probably never see you again after all this. I just want to talk and let all this out. I'm tired of being judged for things I'm not responsible for."

"And what are those things?"

Hassan stays silent for a while, pursing his lips. Meanwhile Dr Johns doesn't look concerned; he keeps his eyes on his patient.

"My parents died when I was very young. Mom was from the Solomon Islands and Dad from Korea. We were extremely poor. One day, I said to Dad that I wanted to go to school. He went to ask the man he worked for to help me. The man insulted him and sent some guys to beat him up. They raped Mom and killed them... in front of me." He falls silent, breathing slowly as if he wanted to stop himself crying.

"You're free to do whatever will help to get better, you can cry or shout if you want," Dr Johns tells him.

Hassan lies on the floor, staring at the ceiling. I'm shaking. What he has said touches me and breaks my heart.

"He never got arrested because he was powerful. Before getting killed, my mother told me to run away. I did it, crying and wondering what my life was going to become. I couldn't save them, and all this was my fault."

"Y—"

"It was not," I say before noticing that I just cut Dr Johns off. I look down, ashamed.

"You can talk. Anyway, I'm not going to charge him. Let's say that it's a talk among friends."

I breathe quietly before talking, "I don't think this is your fault. You couldn't choose your life or your family. No matter what happened after, I think you're so strong for being here alive. You saved them in a way because you're the proof that they existed and loved each other," I tell him, and Dr Johns smiles at me.

"Then I started working on the street, any job was good enough for me. But I'm black and a black Korean isn't something common. People looked at me weirdly, pointing at me, saying I was dirty, making fun of me. This scar, it was one man who was angry because I walked in front of his shop who did that to me."

"The orphanage where I am here, the last headmistress met me one day on the street in Korea and she brought me here. It wasn't easy, but she did it for me. I started trusting people again, because I knew she cared for me. But she died and other people didn't and still don't like me there. In school, they used to throw insults at me. Not just 'black as night' but also 'alien eyes'. They thought it was funny to make jokes about origins or physical appearance. But I don't blame them. Because nowadays it's like that. People will always find a way to hurt you because they think it's funny. They make fun of who you are because they find it funny. I've wanted so many times to die or to change who I am." He stops.

When I close my eyes to hold myself from bursting into tears, images run through my mind. Previously, I have tried several times to clean my skin to remove my skin color. I exercised like crazy to change my body shape. I was called Fifshort, Fifblack and so many other names. They just thought it was fine to make fun of that kind of thing. They had no idea how hurtful it was for me.

"People think that racism is stopping, but I think it's just starting. It's all about whites against Asians and blacks, Asians against blacks and whites, blacks against Asians and whites. It's all about the best-looking race, the best-shaped race, the most intelligent. I'm sick of all this, you know? Why can't we just forget all those superficial things and concentrate on the inside? I love painting but who cares and who even knows it? I love physics and I want to become an Einstein. But who cares?" Hassan continues.

I can't stop any more the tears running down my cheeks any more. How can Dr Johns be so neutral, so calm?

"I tried to talk about it, but then again I've never known whom I could talk to. The only people around me who would have listened, just wanted to argue, not listen to help me", he seems to admit to himself.

The memory of the time I was so broken that I wanted to talk to someone comes to mind. I looked through my phone, searching for the magic friend. But I didn't feeling as comfortable with them as I thought I was. Still, I was sending laughing emojis, and just decided to shut it up once again.

"At some point, I lost myself. I wanted to stop suffering, to kill myself but there again I was thinking about the after. What if God has a plan for me? What if tomorrow is the day everything will stop? Or what if it doesn't even work?"

When he adds that, I see myself again in front of the mirror, crying and staring at the pills in my shaking hands. Then, I see myself throwing them on the floor. I see myself standing at the top of a building, then I see myself breathing harshly and running back to get down. Because no matter how I felt, I wanted to live, I wanted to hope, hope that it would be fine one day.

"Do you want to change to another orphanage?" I suddenly ask him.

"Um, I don't know. I'll turn eighteen in two years. Two years won't kill me I guess."

"I think you should get any opportunity today to get better. I know a place where you'll feel at home. They have children from so many places. You will love it there," I tell him while crying.

Hassan stands up and looks up at me with a smile.

"You would do that for me?"

"Of course, I will, and I'll visit you or you can visit me at any time," I add, wiping my tears.

"Can we go today?" he asks with a shy voice, I nod.

"Of course! As soon as we leave here."

Hassan runs to me, he hugs me like a child but then, he is a child. A child who isn't getting the love he deserves. After Dr Johns has talked with Hassan, we all walk to the lobby. Suddenly, a woman enters, in tears and sobbing. Stacy runs to us and tries to calm her.

"Mrs Potter everything will be fine, we will help you," Dr Johns says softly, squeezing her shoulders. The woman looks instantly calmer.

"He did it again doctor, he did it," she cries. "I can't."

"I'll take her for an extra session, escort her to my office," he tells Stacy before turning to me. "Sorry, I wanted us to discuss about how your internship will work, but…"

"Oh, don't worry, I can come at any time," I say quickly, looking at the woman and Stacy who are walking into the office.

"Well, we'll discuss it tomorrow. Is that all right?"

"After class, I'll be here," I promise him with a confidence I don't actually have. "Do you need any help?" I ask, glancing at the corridor behind him.

"Don't worry. Bye, I have to go."

"Bye Dr Johns." I wave at him.

I turn to Hassan who is leaning against the wall, staring at me. I can't understand why he didn't even shed a tear after those heavy revelations.

"They will be there for the whole evening," he states and we both glance at the corridor before walking out.

I would have never imagined that this job carries that much responsibility. Maybe Dr Johns has some meetings planned, a wife waiting for him at home, maybe she has even cooked his favorite meal. However, he will surely get home very late. The woman looked seriously wrecked. Maybe his children are waiting for him, to do homework with them or even to tell them a bedtime tale, before they go to sleep, but they are not getting that today. He surely has a private life, but he has to sacrifice it for his patients. If he had left that woman and told her to go home and come another time, he would have seemed like a bad psychologist.

"How did you get here?" I ask Hassan once we step onto the parking lot.

"I walked," he quietly answers.

"You walked? From where?" I exclaim.

"From the orphanage."

"Wow…" I clear my throat. "Get in the car, and we will collect your things."

We get in the car and I start driving; Hassan is skipping through the stations to find some music. He stops on one that's definitely not my kind of music. He gives me the address. I connect my phone to the radio and put on some Shawn Mendes' music. Hassan gives me a look that says *Like seriously?*

"What?"

"Well, you do definitely look like a girl who listens to Mendes," he observes while watching the landscape. I glance at him before looking back at the road.

"What do you mean? What does a girl who listens to Shawn Mendes looks like?"

"You," he answers playfully, I roll my eyes.

At a crossroad, I almost forget to look before pulling out. I stop the car at the last second before crashing into another one. I see the lady in the other car shouting and I quickly drive away to escape her venom.

"If you want us to die, they are so many better ways," Hassan observes, amused.

"And what do you know about the different ways to die?" I tease him but he abruptly looks away.

I can't believe that I just said that. How stupid am I to ask such an uncomfortable question to someone who just told me about the way he has been thinking about suicide before! The temperature seemed to drop between us at my reply. We fall silent, except for "Bad Reputation" by Shawn Mendes that's playing. Hassan is humming the song while staring at the landscape.

"I thought you didn't like him," I tease him, he blushes slightly.

"I never said that. I just said that you look like a fan," he defends himself. I smile at his discomfort.

"Do you have a girlfriend?" I suddenly ask him; he looks surprised.

"Do I look like someone who has a girlfriend?" he replies, narrowing his eyes.

I roll my eyes. "I'd like to know how you class people in each of those categories. Well, do I look like a psychologist?"

"No." His answer strikes my heart, making me stop breathing. "You look like a friend, someone we'd like to have in our life. Someone we'd love to talk to," he adds.

"I don't know if this is a good thing or not," I say nervously.

"You don't look like a psychologist, but you would be a great one," he says kindly.

"Thank you."

We finally arrive at the orphanage. Most of the young people there are teenagers and most of them don't look happy at all. They are all staring at us.

"Before she died, this place was paradise," Hassan sighs sadly.

"We'll take your stuff. For the paperwork and all the legal side, Shawn will manage."

"Who's Shawn?"

"My boyfriend."

"You're that obsessed with Mendes?" he exclaims playfully, making me roll my eyes.

"It has nothing to do with Shawn Mendes," I defend myself. Yet, it's funny that my boyfriend has the same name as my favorite singer.

Hassan smirks but ends up shrugging. "Okay, I'll get my stuff quickly before Mrs Janklin sees us and starts on one of her long speeches. I just want to leave here," he whines, making me laugh.

He walks quickly inside, leaving me alone in the huge courtyard. I am staring at all the children. They are alone even though some people act like they care, but each of these children is just a charity case to them, an insignificant piece of a big effort. Meanwhile, they are all dreaming of being special. I scan the place, secretly wishing happiness for each of them. Hassan reappeared and has been talking with a red-haired girl, who seems nice. He is talking to her cautiously while she is crying. He smoothes her hair and hugs her, his backpack on his back. I watch the scene carefully till he joins me and the girl disappears.

"Is that all what you're taking?" I ask him.

"I travel light," he replies casually.

Before we leave the place, his eyes meet the girl's eyes once again; he looks down.

During the drive, I try to bring the subject up, "You're not the girlfriend type, huh?"

"She's not. She just... She just likes me," he splutters, avoiding eyes contact.

"And you don't like her?"

He looks away. "I've started talking with her recently. She's the one who told me to see Dr Johns. I told her that I will visit her as much as I can."

"Didn't she want to follow you?"

Hassan frowns. "Would you do that for her too?"

"Yeah. I mean, if we can manage to get some children out of that scary place. I have seen their faces. They looked so sad," I observe, a sour taste in my mouth.

"I can tell you. Theresa is so scared of leaving, I don't know if she would like to face Mrs Janklin." I squeeze his thigh gently and smile at him.

"We will do this. You'll see. Everything will work out in the end. Your last couple of years in high school are going to be better."

"Fifa?" he says shyly.

"Mmm?"

"How were your high school years?"

His question makes my blood run cold in my veins. I remember that special moment of my senior year. I liked a boy so much, and he acted like he liked me. I promised myself that I wouldn't make the same mistake with him as with my first boyfriend, Connor. I acted like a normal girl. I showed him poems I wrote, not knowing that he was making fun of them behind my back and showing them to his friends. He just wanted to find out what it was like to date a girl like me. I feel so ashamed of it that I can't even talk about it to Shawn. Him and his friends were making fun of my loss, my depression. They didn't really care about me; they just thought it was easy to get through sad things.

"It was fine," I say smiling.

***

When we enter the large room, the difference between this orphanage and the other one is clear. There are different areas: one looks like a video game area, another one is a dance area and there is even one for writing. The decoration is absolutely amazing. Hassan is looking around, clearly amazed. We enter the room where Shawn works. He is talking to some kids with an incredible smile on his face. They are really attentive to his words. When he spots us, he walks over to us with them following.

"I want each of you to tell me afterwards what you found out, okay?" he says loudly to them.

"Yes Shawn," they say before running away.

"They are doing an orientation exercise to find out what they like and what they are really good at," he explains to us.

"I love this," I tell him, smiling. His eyes land on Hassan. "So, this is Hassan. I told you about him on phone," I add, wrapping my arm around his shoulder.

"Yes, nice to meet you Hassan, I'm Shawn," he says and they shake hands.

"Fifa talked about you so much that I feel like I already know you," he answers. I elbow him in the side, making both of them chuckle.

"I like your humor," Shawn says. "Come, let's sit. I'm done for today anyway."

We sit down.

"So, this a classroom?" I ask, looking around.

"Kind of. Here we talk about how to be happy, how to live. It's a discussion class for the under twelves," Shawn answers. "How old are you?"

"Sixteen."

"Great. I'll introduce you to the headmistress and we'll see what to do. She'll get in contact with your orphanage and they will work everything out," Shawn explains to us.

"What about his friends?" I ask, seeing Hassan's sudden shyness.

"Well… If we succeed in showing that they are really not well treated over there, we can manage to get some of them here or in other orphanages."

We meet the headmistress, a sweet young lady. After all the paperwork, I say goodbye to Hassan before driving to my place. Shawn says he will join me soon. My mother has a night shift, and my father is in L.A. for the week. I take a quick shower and put on some comfortable clothes. I make dinner for Shawn and me. He finally rings the doorbell. It feels like I've not seen him in ages, and I run to open the door.

"Hey," he says before pressing his lips to mine.

"Hey."

He enters then we go to the kitchen. "Hassan said that you were incredible today," Shawn says. I smile while putting boiled yams with meat sauce on his plate.

"Today was a wow day," I remark, still taken aback by all that happened in one day. I serve myself before sitting down.

"He's settling in well. And about that girl, she will join him next week," Shawn adds before popping a bite of yam into his mouth. "This is nice"."

"He told you about her?" I ask, surprised.

"Yes. He's told me everything."

"Teach me your ways," I groan before we laugh.

"A master doesn't show his cards," he proudly replies.

After dinner, Shawn and I clean up, putting the plates in the dishwasher and washing the glasses. We go in the hot tub after all that. The hot tub is in a wooden room, with a huge bay window that gives a wonderful view of the sky. We are sitting next to each other, staring up.

"Did I tell you that you're incredibly sexy in that underwear?" he whispers playfully against my ear, making me blush.

"At least hundred time," I assure him; he smirks.

"Let me say it again and again." He turns my head to him and kisses me gently. The heat grows in my stomach, I kiss him back. I climb in his lap, wrap my arms around his neck. "Mmm, sexy..." he whispers, making me giggle. His hands are on my waist, pulling me closer to him.

"Call me Miss Sexy," I simper jokingly. His turn to giggle.

After a while, I let my head fall on his shoulder. He slowly walks his fingers up and down on my back.

"You smell good," I whisper.

The sound of the doorbell makes me flinch. I start to get up to open the door.

"Don't bother yourself, let me go," Shawn says, already leaving the hot tub.

I really don't want to stand up, so I just let him go.

"Shawn?" I call. He turns to me. "You should maybe use the towel." He smiles.

"Okay, ma'am."

He wraps himself with the towel before walking out. Minutes later he comes back, I look up at him. "Who was it?"

"Chester, the Magnificent," I hear Chester answer loudly from behind me. My eyes go wide as I look around to find something to cover my body. I put my arms over my chest. Chester is now standing next to Shawn, in front of me. He starts removing his clothes.

"What... what are you doing?" I stammer, frowning.

"Come on. You guys aren't having a romantic kind of night, are you?" he says without waiting for an answer. I roll my eyes, annoyed.

"Maybe are we," I reply irritated.

"Kate, are you coming?"

"Kate?" I repeat but Chester ignores me.

I breathe slowly to get control of myself. I tell myself that by killing him, I will just end up in jail. And maybe he would follow me in my nightmares. Kate walks in, already in her underwear.

"Thank you so much for inviting us" she thanks me; I frown.

"What? Wait I didn't invite anyone," I snap, indignant. I feel like I missed something.

"Shawn said that he was hanging out at your place this evening. Then I remembered seeing this amazing hot tub around here, so I just invited myself and Kate," Chester explains casually.

"If there is a problem, we can just leave," Kate says uncomfortably.

"You can stay, Kate," I sigh but smile at her. "Chester is the only one disturbing us," I add, glaring at him.

Chester puts his arm around Kate's shoulder and smiles to me. "I know you guys can't live without me."

We all burst out laughing as Shawn enters the hot tub. He sits down by me, pulls me closer to him and kisses my hair. We spend the evening talking and laughing.

CHAPTER TWENTY-THREE

After school, I go to Dr Johns' office. There he gives me my schedule and tells me what my internship with involve. When I ask him about the woman from yesterday, he assures that she will be fine. In the evening, I cook with my mother before Shawn and Frida arrive for dinner.

"I think that's a great idea!" my mother exclaims after drinking a bit of water.

"A family vacation... that sounds so good," Frida adds dreamily.

"Come on, you guys are already planning the summer vacation," Shawn grouses looking down at his plate.

"He's right. I don't know if I'll last till then, let's just think about winter," Frida says calmly. She doesn't look at all sad though. I stay silent and eat my soup.

"Don't say that, Grandma, you still have years ahead," Shawn chides her coldly.

"Ronel has a nice chalet. Maybe could we go there for Christmas?" suggests my mother.

"I'd love it," Frida replies hastily.

Shawn and I stay silent for the remaining of the dinner. He looks preoccupied, and I guess that it's about what Frida said. Frida stays in the living room with my mother; they will probably spend the evening talking unless my mother gets called out to the hospital. Shawn and I finally catch up with our romantic night in the hot tub. Over the next few days, Shawn often comes to my house.

Today, we are lying on my bed, talking about nothing and everything. He says that Hassan is a good guy and that he is always helping others. Hassan says that he is happy to be surrounded by people from all over the world. He says that he still feels different, but that seeing that they are all different and that they are helped to accept it, makes him feel like he is part of something. He has already subscribed to the painting workshop of the orphanage. He already has some fans because he paints very well. He is the next Leonardo da Vinci. Then, Shawn gives me a painting of me that Hassan did. I am so pleased and honored that tears flow down my cheeks.

I call Hassan to thank him and we talk for a while. Shawn helps me to put the portrait on the wall right next to my mirror.

"How do you feel?" Shawn asks me in a soft tone as we sit by the window.

"Well," I smile at him. "What about you?" I ask back gently.

"I always feel well," he answers with his usual smile.

"Yeah, that's the problem," I observe, narrowing my eyes. He looks away as he tenses. "I mean... you know that you're not meant to always feel well? You have the right to —"

"Please, let's not talk about this," he stops me abruptly.

I squeeze his hand, smile at him before raining kisses onto his hands. "I'll always be there for you," I promise him.

***

"Are you coming home tonight?" My mother asks as I grab my bag.

"No, Mom," I answer, walking to the door.

"Be careful and protect yourself," she adds playfully, making me groan.

"Mom, stop," I whine as she giggles.

"What? I'm just being a mother," she defends herself.

I roll my eyes before walking back to kiss and hug her. She has just got back from the hospital; she looks exhausted. These last few days, my parents have been weird. I don't know what they're keeping from me. Besides, mother has been even more preoccupied than usual lately. I walk out of the house and drive to Shawn's for our movie night with Frida. We have been planning this for weeks, but we haven't got the chance to do it before now. I brought some cakes made of groundnut from Benin that Frida likes so much. The light is on in Shawn's room and downstairs. I ring the bell and a minute later, he opens the door to me.

"Hello, Miss Lawson." He leans against the door with his arm.

"Hello Mr Davis."

"We're being such a weird couple," he remarks as I am entering the lobby. Obviously, I giggle.

"Old fashioned, I guess."

He helps me to remove my coat before I turn to him to press my lips against his. He takes my bag from me and we enter the living room. Frida is already sitting on the couch, blankets around her and snacks all over the table. I put down the one I brought and hug her tightly.

"Fifa, I'm so glad to have you with us tonight," she says. She delicately kisses me on the cheeks.

"So, am I. Are you ready?"

"Yes!" she exclaims. I giggle at her energy.

"I'll be right back."

I go up to Shawn's room, where he has put my bag around his bed. He is doing something on his laptop.

"What are you doing?"

"I forgot to choose the Netflix series and movies that we're going to watch," he explains to me. I stand behind him, massaging his shoulders.

"I love that one," I tell him, pointing at the title.

"'13 Reasons Why? Seriously? We're having a funny movie night, remember?"

"What? I like it," I reply hastily.

"I also do, but I just want light and funny things tonight," he answers.

"What are you trying to forget or escape from?" I ask him feeling nosy and concerned. He raises an eyebrow at me.

"Geez, nothing. I just want to laugh," he snaps, on the defensive.

"Are you guys coming?" we hear Frida shout from downstairs.

"Yeah, Grandma," Shawn shouts back, taking his laptop. He walks to the door and looks at me. "Are you coming?"

"Sure," I sigh.

"We're going to start with 'The Big Bang Theory' and then move onto some Netflix movies and finish with cartoons," Shawn announces as we sit down.

We both sit on another couch, blankets over our laps. We start finally with an episode of the tenth season of "The Big Bang Theory" with audio description. It's the episode in which Bernadette is pregnant and has to tell Howard. They are arguing about the fact that she's pregnant. We laugh at each reply.

"How can they be surprised? They have sex all the time," Shawn observes before taking a handful of popcorn that he pops into his mouth.

"Maybe they use protection," I suggest.

"Come on, they are married," he replies.

"Maybe he was not ready. Kids are evil," Frida teases. We laugh, Shawn takes a long sip of his drink as I eat some popcorn and Frida concentrates on the groundnut cakes.

"I was not evil," Shawn replies, shrugging.

"You were the representative of Satan, I can tell you," she grouses, making me laugh.

"Bullshit."

After a few episodes of "The Big Bang Theory" later, we watch "Sierra Burgess is a Loser" and finally watch some "Tom and Jerry". I'm lying on my side on the couch with Shawn lying on his back. My head is on his chest, I can hear his heart beating fast and even the deep sound of his laugh sometimes.

"Shawn is Tom," I tease him.

"I'm not."

"Frida, tell him that he's Tom."

But she doesn't answer. Shawn and I look at each other before straightening. Frida is not sleeping; her eyes are open and she is sitting upright but looks absent. Shawn looks at me and then walks to her while I am kneeling on the couch. He sits next to her, turns her head to him.

"Grandma? Are you okay?" She doesn't answer, Shawn starts to worry. "Not again," he snaps loudly, making me flinch.

He gets up off the couch, makes her lie down and covers her body with the blanket. I am paralyzed, not able to move. Shawn looks upset. He kisses her gently on the forehead, walks to the TV to turn it off.

185

"What's going on?" I ask him.

"Nothing," he answers, walking out of the house.

I glance at Frida; her eyes are still open and she is breathing but not moving. I walk out too and spot Shawn sitting on a bench on the porch. It's very cold so I rub my arms with my hands to keep warm. I sit by him and gently take his hand in mine. I slowly rub my thumb on the back of his hand.

"Sometimes, she just gets absent like that'," he starts with a shaky voice. "I'm scared of what this means. The doctor said that it is her disease," Shawn continues quietly, trying to stop himself from crying. He removes his hand from mine to run it over his face. "I'm not ready for this... I'm not ready to lose her too," he confesses with a broken voice that breaks my heart into millions of pieces.

I don't know how to act. I don't know how it feels to have lost all my family and to be on the verge of losing the only one remaining. I don't know that pain and I wish he had never known it either. "Shawn..." This is the only thing that comes out of my mouth when I open it. I am afraid that Frida is the only reason why he is still holding on. I am afraid of what might happen if he loses her. I am afraid of Shawn trying so hard to be happy while in reality he is running away from sadness; he is just hiding from himself. "Everything will be fine. She'll be fine."

Shawn's body is shaking but he is not crying. I kneel down in front of him and hug him tightly. I slowly walk my hand across his back. We stay in that position for minutes, without moving, just he and I, trying to give a sense to life. After all, what is life? What is it except a succession of hurt, injuries and failure and then, success and joy? Is it just the time before death, or is it the time to prepare us for it? Is Frida ready for death? She seemed to be, the last time. But are we ever ready to die? Ready to wipe away our presence on Earth? And the most painful question... Are we ever ready to lose someone? Can we be ready to never again be able to see them smile, cry, speak or even exist? Shawn seems to not be ready to lose Frida. Somehow, I know that he will never be ready for it.

CHAPTER TWENTY-FOUR

*H*appiness *tip eleven: Stop worrying about the future.*
That is the tip Shawn sent me a couple weeks
ago. Since then, no more tips. He is doing better since
what happened with Frida and apparently, she is doing
well too. That night, Shawn and I went to his room after
cleaning up and locking up the house. We slept in each
other's arms; our silence was full of promises. Promise
that neither of us has the right to abandon the other, that
we have to be honest with each other. The week that
followed, everything went back to normal, with Chester
being annoying and Shawn being lovely. Chester and
Kate claim to just be friends, but I would bet that they
are much more than that. The way Chester looks at her
is different; he looks at her as if she is the only person he
wants in his life.

Hassan's friend has joined him. They are starting their
new life. My internship at Dr Johns' office goes on twice a
week and sometimes Saturday too. I don't have the right
to attend to the sessions after Hassan's, but I learn many
things about the job and… somehow… about myself.
Before, I would never have thought that I could do
something like this: talk to people, give them advice and
be there for them. Before, I never trusted anyone enough
to open myself up. I guess, today I should start. I guess,
it's time to close that chapter of my life and start over, and
start to be me… And start to live.

Shawn is spending much more time with Frida than he used to. He looks permanently scared when it comes to her. I think he wants to enjoy as much time with her as possible before she leaves, forever. Not die, just leave. Because that is not death. Death is something horrible that takes someone's life, that tears everything apart: dreams, hope, family, life. Death is horrible. Frida is just going to travel; she's going to a better place.

Once, I invited Hassan and his friend at home to join our family dinner — Shawn and Frida are now part of our family. He is different from the Hassan I first met; he is happier. In such a short time he has changed, or maybe he became who he really is. It's so sad how we can lose ourselves when life is not fair to us. Hassan looks so happy about finishing high school in two years and wants to go to an art college and become an artist. He is also planning on doing a minor in physics or even a major if he gets the time for it. He has dreams that he would have never thought, years ago, he would be able to achieve. What would have happened to him if that woman had never found him in the first place? What if his parents had never died? Does everything happen for a purpose?

If I hadn't lived through that awful thing years ago, would I have got the chance to meet Shawn? Or would everything be different? Only God knows that.

***

Today is Thanksgiving, well in the United States. My family has always preferred to celebrate it after Halloween. We are hosting Shawn, Frida, Hassan and Theresa. Tom, Caroline and Liam are having Thanksgiving dinner at Tom's. Chester invited Kate to his parents' house in

Ottawa. The twins said that it's the first time they are going to spend Thanksgiving separately. I came back from the grocery store hours ago; the turkey is ready — Mother has a secret recipe — and everywhere smells like heaven. I have decorated the table with a green and copper color palette, craft paper cards on which I wrote nice words for each person coming and put them neatly on their plates. And the final touch, small pumpkins all over the table.

We have spent hours cooking the food because for the first time, we are receiving people. My father's parents live in Benin, and they hate travelling. Besides, there is no Thanksgiving over there. My mother's dad died years ago but mother is not really on good terms with her own mother. She's been invited twice, but we don't invite her any more because of all the remarks she makes. She's kind of unbearable. So, we are used to spending Thanksgiving just the three of us. As this year we are getting loving guests, we want it to be perfect. Father took out champagne and his best wines. I am wearing a V-neck traditional jumpsuit made of traditional fabric from Benin, with heels covered with the same fabric. The necklace that Shawn's given to me is hanging around my neck and falling exactly to the top of my breasts. For once, I decide to let my long frizzy hair free. I look at myself in the mirror for several minutes; I like how womanly I look.

"You're beautiful; you look like an African beauty," Mother gushes as soon as I get downstairs.

"Thank you, Mom, you look nice too," I answer her warmly, hugging her.

We put the food on the large table in the dining room. We hardly eat there, except when father's colleagues come for dinner. Dad puts on some old music in the living room; the music fills the ground floor.

"I think we're going to have leftovers for days. Welcome to sandwiches for every meal," I tease Mother, making her roll her eyes.

But I am only half joking. We made roasted butternut squash with cider vinaigrette; wild rice and cider-cranberry pilaf; sage butter roasted turkey and mashed potatoes. For dessert, I prepared cast iron apple-blackberry crumble while Mother made pie-spiced apple fritters. As soon as the bell rings, I run to open the door. I discover Shawn and Frida in their Sunday clothes, standing on the porch. Shawn has once again tried to comb his hair neatly but I bet it will soon be a total mess.

"Oh shit!" Shawn sucks in a breath while looking me up and down, mouth open. I love having that effect on him. It makes me feel special. "You're... oh God," he stutters, wide eyes, making me chuckle.

"Don't have a heart attack," I tease him before kissing him on the cheek, but he presses his lips to mine and I smile.

"I guess you're beautiful," Frida speaks up. I give her a bright smile (even though she can't see it) before pulling her in for a hug.

"Welcome. Nice to see you," I tell her.

Hassan and Theresa have just arrived. They are both wearing grey, this is so cute.

"You drive now?" I ask Hassan, looking over his shoulder.

"Hello, I'm doing well too," he starts teasingly, making me roll my eyes. "And yes, just got it. Do you like it?" he adds as we all take a look at the car.

"It's all right. How are you, my dear?" I ask Theresa, giving her a welcoming smile.

"Fine and you? Thank you for inviting us." She has such a wonderful, but quiet, voice. She is sweet. Hassan has a good taste.

"I'm fine. You're really pretty," I say to her. She thanks me politely. "Come in."

We all walk to the dining room.

"You guys have a dining room, but you always eat in the kitchen?" Shawn remarks, but as soon as he realizes that he was thinking aloud, he blushes slightly. I decide not to intervene and let him be embarrassed in front of my parents for once. He's too perfect. Maybe am I the devil. *Mwahaha.* I giggle at my thoughts, earning a glare from Shawn. I reply with a wink, at which he shakes his head, smiling.

We sit around the table, chatting. I am sitting between Shawn and Hassan. Next to Hassan, there is Theresa who is sitting right next to my mother and my father. Frida is just at the right of Shawn. "Before we eat, I wrote a few words for each of you," I tell them, pointing out the small cards. "You have to take them and read them at home," I specify.

"Sweet little brother," Hassan starts, earning a glare and a snatch from me.

"I said home," I remind him, and he smirks.

I am glad to see him doing so much better and I hope all those bad memories will soon be in the past or that they already are. I glance discreetly at Shawn who smiles at me. He reads what I wrote under the table. The way his face lights up makes my heart flutter. The way he looks up at me after reading it just drives me crazy. I don't even know what do with all these feelings I have for him, except accept them and live with them, as much as I can. It's a family atmosphere as we eat, laughing and talking. Hassan is eating for four people though. At the dessert time, he leans against the chair, patting his stomach.

"Oh, I'm full," he whines.

"Wonder why. Chester and you should really get along," I tease him, serving Shawn who is looking at us, amused. He sticks his tongue out at me. "Are you really turning seventeen? You act like a small child," I tease him again, sucking the sugar off my fingers.

"You always do that to Shawn, so we are both children," he replies, stealing something from my plate.

I dramatically put my hand on my heart. "Touché."

After dinner, mother gets an emergency call from the hospital, so she has to leave. Frida and Dad move to the living room to talk about architecture. Hassan and Theresa leave after I give them some leftovers to take with them. Shawn and I head to my room. As soon as I enter, I slip my shoes off my feet. We sit by the window as usual. His eyes are on my necklace, the one he gave me. "I love your necklace," he says with a small smile at the corner of his lips.

"Really?" I decide to play along with his game.

"Sure, Miss Lawson," he replies and we laugh. "Where did you find that?"

"From..." I come closer to him, our gazes are connected. I continue in a very soft and seductive tone, "my amazing..." I kiss him on the forehead; "boyfriend," I kiss him on the nose.

"Hmm? What is he like?" he continues in a way that could kill me.

"Stupid..." I kiss him on the right cheek, giggling. "Handsome." I kiss him on the left cheek.

"I think so," he agrees and it's my turn to laugh.

"And great, lovely... and mine," I add before kissing him on the lips. He runs his hands through my hair and pulls me closer to him while kissing me harder. "I like you so much," I confess to him.

"I know," he teases me. I hit him on the shoulder and push him away. He falls on the floor dramatically and I laugh. "Can't we joke any more?" he complains in an amused voice.

I sit, crossing my legs while he is standing, my palms on the bench. "Not with feelings," I state and he leans in to kiss me.

"Okay, ma'am. I do like you too."

"You'd better."

We laugh again. We sit again. I decide to ask him a question that I've been holding in for weeks, "Shawn?"

"Mmm?"

"Have you... have you ever thought about the next level?" I ask him uncomfortably.

He furrows his brows. "What do you mean?" he asks, clueless.

"I mean have you ever... " I clear my throat. "Thought about having sex?"

"Have you?" he asks back.

"I asked first," I snap.

"So, you want to know if I've already fucked someone or thought about it?" he says with playful smirk. I roll my eyes.

"Shawn, language!" I caution him; he chuckles.

"Mother used to speak like you 'Shawn language!'," he observes while laughing and I laugh too. "And the worse is that Chester would say 'Yeah, Shawn, your fucking language' and mother would get mad." Then we burst out laughing before he speaks again. "Well, I don't know how you will take it but I'm one of those old-fashioned guys. I want to wait till marriage," he confesses. My eyes go wide.

"Really?"

"Yes. I know it's kind of weird for an almost twenty-year-old boy, but I guess we all have the right to decide about our own bodies." He pauses, "But I kind of sometimes, like rarely but sometimes, satisfy myself," he adds uncomfortably, shifting on the seat.

I'm so relieved about the first part of his speech that I hug him. I have been so stressed about this, about the fact that Shawn would want more than I do.

"For information, I'm hugging you for the first part," I specify while chuckling.

"What? You're a virgin?" he asks me.

I narrowed my eyes at him to know if he is kidding me or not, but he seems serious.

"What do you think? The only other relationship I've ever been in was a total mess. And yes, I'm waiting too, at least till I'm into something really serious and all. Like long-term. Like after months and months. Like…"

"Okay, I got it," he stops me, laughing.

We spend the remaining of the evening talking.

CHAPTER TWENTY-FIVE

I'm standing on the driveway. Shawn and Frida are in the car, going back to their house. I wave at Shawn who smiles to me. He starts the car but looks at something down. I don't know how it happens but he seems to lose control. The car speeds up; I back away but I feel it running over my feet. I scream. My head hits the pole behind me. I lean against it to handle the pain. I hear the car door close and then Shawn's hand lands on my shoulder.

"I'm sorry, so sorry. Are you fine? Let's go to the hospital. This fucking car needs repairing," he says panicked.

"No, I'm fine," I sigh and straighten up but everything starts spinning around me. Then, black out.

***

My eyes slowly open and I look around. White walls. I touch my head, there are bandages around it and around my feet. Then, I remember what just happened. A nurse enters. "Miss Lawson, are you awake?"

"Yes. Where's Shawn?" I ask in a really low voice.

"Your boyfriend? He's talking with the doctor."

"And, is there anything wrong?" I continue, worried about the answer.

"I—"

The door opens and I see my mother enter. "Mom."

"Thank you, Anne, I'll take care of her." The nurse walks out. "Shawn is feeling guilty but don't worry. You're fine, you'll be back home tomorrow," she says with her doctor voice, not her mother one. But when she gently strokes my cheek, like a mother, I feel better.

"Can I see him?" I ask weakly.

"Sure, let me call him. I've to go back to work. You'll need to rest after this, okay?"

"Okay, Mom." She kisses me lightly on both cheeks.

Minutes later, Shawn enters, he looks tired. I frown. "What's wrong?"

"I could have killed you," he groans through a whisper and looks away.

"No. And this is not your fault, Shawn," I reassure him, pulling him by the sleeve of his shirt.

"It is. I've had some problems with the car for days. I should have had it fixed as soon as it started. Then I wouldn't have hurt you," he says while rubbing his thumb on my bottom lip.

"I said this is not your fault, Shawn. I'm fine, okay? Kiss me and I will be even better," I add and smile at him. "Kiss me, Shawn," I order.

He leans in to kiss me. After, he goes back to check on Frida and I get visited by my father.

Today, I am leaving the hospital. After putting on my clothes and tying my hair in a bun, I grab my bag and leave the room after the nurse leaves. I slowly walk across the corridors to wait for Shawn in the lobby; he is obviously using my car. He will get his back today. My feet are not hurting too much, so I can walk almost normally. Since there are too many people in the main hallway, I decide to take a shortcut. I know this hospital like the back of my hand because when I was younger,

I used to hang out here as Mother always worked late. I sometimes used to think that my parents wouldn't last because they don't seem that in love, but I guess I was wrong. They are just typical African parents we never see kissing. I suddenly hear something fall and laughter in one of the rooms nearby. I want to just keep on my way but I hear my mother laugh. "You're so clumsy" she says as she giggles.

"You make me clumsy," a man's voice says; my heart stops beating.

I stop in the middle of the corridor, looking around, waiting to wake up as if this is a nightmare, but nothing changes. I still hear moans and laughter. I step back and I stand on tiptoe, a lump in my throat. The beating of my heart is painful. I look through the round window in the door and see my mother, leaning against the desk and kissing a doctor, as if she were not married, as if she were not a mother, as if she were a slut. And the worse is that the man's face looks familiar; I know him. I don't know how to feel. I don't know if I am hurt or disappointed or just surprised. Of all the people in this world, I would have never imagined that my mother would do something like that, cheat on her husband. She's left her patients and her family and here she is with another man.

I want to vomit, to scream and to cry. The only role-model I ever had is just a kind of slut cheating on her husband and lying to her family. My eyes are hurting me; I want to act. I want to break into that room and shout at her, spit on them and tell her how much I hate her right now but I can't move.

"You should go back to work," she tells him, but he shuts her up with a kiss. I nervously run my hand over my hair before walking quickly to escape, to leave there, to walk and walk and never see her again. I'm so disgusted.

When I step into the lobby, Shawn is standing by some couches. As soon as he sees me, he walks over to me but looks worried after looking at me carefully. I'm breathing heavily; I've even almost forgotten the pain in my feet.

"Are you okay? Is anywhere hurting you?" he asks me, frowning.

"I just want to leave here," I breathe out, holding myself from crying.

At each step, I feel so many things happening inside me. The images of my mother with another man is playing through my mind, again and again. I always come to her for advice and this is who she really is. When she calls me, I don't answer. Then she sends me a message asking me if I arrived home okay. I don't want to reply. I show the prescription to Shawn who stops by a pharmacy to pick up the drugs.

I know Shawn is glancing at me all the way home but I don't dare to look at him. I feel like crying but no tears fall on my cheek. "My mother is cheating on my dad." The sentence leaves my mouth when he stops on the driveway of my house.

I turn to him, analyzing his shocked expression. Mother looks so perfect, so irreproachable that even after seeing it I still can't believe it.

"What do you mean?" Shawn asks, frowning. "I mean… are you sure of what you're saying?"

"I am. I just saw her kissing one of her colleagues. And I know the man. He used to offer candies to me when I was little. Can you imagine that?" I wonder how I can stay this calm after everything. "All the time, he's just been thinking about having her in his bed," I say quietly, hurt.

"Wow... I don't really know what to say..." He nervously scratches his temple.

"Don't worry. I don't know either. Don't you just want me to hang out at your place today?" I look up at him with sad eyes.

"Sure."

If I were not so confused by my mother's behavior, I would have made fun of Shawn about the fact that he agrees just because I'm kind of giving him a ride home but I don't have energy for that right now. When we arrive at his place, Frida is in the kitchen, having her breakfast. I think about walking straight to Shawn's room but I know she smells my perfume.

"Hello, Frida," I say with a fake happy voice.

"Oh, Fifa, I'm so sorry about yesterday. I dropped something on the floor and..."

"It's fine," I cut her off warmly. "I will see you later."

When we enter Shawn's room, I sit on his bed, thinking about what to do. I don't even have the strength to tell my father. Shawn sits at the foot of the bed, staring at me as if he was afraid of talking.

"I'm sorry. If this hadn't happened, you wouldn't have seen that," he starts uncomfortably.

"And what? And never know this? I'm glad to have seen it," I almost shout. I lean against the head of the bed, stretching my legs out in front of me. Shawn puts one of my hurt legs on his thigh and massages it slowly. It is just slightly painful but also good. There is a photo on the bed, I grab it after glancing at Shawn. It is a young brown-haired girl; she looks sick in all honesty. Her eyelids are hollow, her body lean. Paradoxically though, she has a huge, warm smile. The kind of smile that makes you smile back. "Mia?"

"Yeah."

I look at the photo for a long time. "You miss her, don't you?" I ask him with a low voice.

Shawn exhales. "I miss all of them. But I can't live in the past."

I nod, watching him. I kneel down on the bed to hug him tightly. He wraps his arms around me, pulls me closer to him.

***

It has been one week since I saw my mother with that man. And I am still pissed off and sad and disappointed. I have been avoiding her ever since; I can't even look into her eyes; she disgusts me. My father asks me why I am behaving like that but I can't tell him. I don't want to hurt him. But isn't that what I am doing right now? Whether he discovers it sooner or later, he will still be hurt and probably mad that I've been hiding it from him. And this is in fact what I am doing. But how to say to your dad that his wife is cheating on him? How can you tell him that the only woman you ever respected is a slut?

My internship is going well so far, Dr Johns has been asking me questions, but I respectfully tell him that I am not a patient. Chester tries to figure out what is going on but I can't tell him; I am so ashamed.

It's Saturday. I have just finished bathing after jogging with Shawn. I am working in the kitchen. My mother enters. I ignore her, praying that she leaves fast.

"Hello, darling, how are you?" she asks with her hypocritical smile, but I don't answer. How can she have this peace of mind? "Enough," she says firmly, then softens her voice. "What's wrong, Fifame? Is it Shawn who did something to you?"

"Shawn? You think Shawn has anything to do with this?" I can't keep my mouth shut any more. "And what? You're going to give me some advice while your own life is bullshit?" My voice is loud, very loud and I can't keep calm. She backs away, worried and surprised.

"W-what are you talking about?" she stutters, blinking.

"What's going on here?" My dad enters the kitchen looking tired. I glare at my mother.

"Ask your wife," I snap, gathering my things to walk out.

"I don't know what's going on. She's been pissed off for days for no reason," she stammers. I laugh nervously.

"No reason? What about the fact that I saw you with that man, kissing and cuddling?" I scream and she gasps.

My father sighs, "Fifa. This is not what you think."

"Aren't you mad at her? Are you serious?" I can't believe this. I am nervously shaking my head.

"Your mother and I have divorced for a month," he announces. I feel like the earth is opening under my feet and eating me.

"What?"

"We're still good friends but not a couple any more," he continues while mother says silent. "We wanted to tell you after everything is sorted out but…"

"I can't believe this. You guys were pretending to be together in front of me while preparing your divorce, without telling me? Your daughter?"

"We didn't want to worry you, or…" he tries to say.

"Or what? You didn't want me to be depressed? How could you hide something like that from me? I'm not a kid any more and I would have understood your choice. But not this. You're insane."

I walk out of the kitchen. I need fresh air.

"Wait please," my mother calls to me but I can't stop. I don't want to listen to them. I get in my car, hands shaking, and start the engine. They are outside, watching me leave, paralyzed. Tears are flowing down my cheeks. I am so hurt. I drive to Shawn's. I press on the doorbell like the devil; he finally comes to open it. As soon as his eyes land on me, he knows something is wrong. I just throw myself into his arm, crying and sobbing.

"Shush. I'm here," he says softly but I can't stop.

This is the worst thing I could have learned. My parents lied to me; they are divorced. Not even going to divorce — already divorced. They were acting for me, the same way I did with them. But at least, I did it for them. But they are just selfish.

CHAPTER TWENTY-SIX

When I enter the house, I spot Chester and Kate sitting on the couch, but Frida is nowhere to be found. Maybe she is sleeping. Chester and Kate give me worried looks but don't speak.

"Hey," I greet them with a small smile, wiping my tears.

"Hi Fif," they both say.

"Can I watch it with you?" I ask them, pointing at the TV.

I don't really want to just sit somewhere, mourning over what my parents did to me. I just want to live my life and keep on. I sit on a couch with Shawn. We watch movies all day. Tomorrow I will surely shut myself in my room to work all day for the next exams.

Sunday, Shawn calls me in the morning, but he doesn't bring up the situation with my parents. I told the team the whole story about my parents, they were all as astonished as I am. In the evening, I finally leave my room because I am starving. As soon as I step into the living room to go through to the kitchen, I regret it. My mother is sitting on the couch and my father has just entered. I want to walk away but he calls me, "Please Fifa, we need to talk."

I breathe slowly and walk to the kitchen, grab plantain chips and a big bottle of apple juice before heading back to the living room. I sit and pop some chips into my mouth, chewing them slowly to keep calm. If they want me to listen to any excuses they have right now, I need something to eat.

"So, talk," I speak up, looking away.

My father sits next to my mother. "Well…"

"I don't want to listen to her. Daddy, talk," I cut her off; she looks hurt but I don't really care. He clears his throat.

"We didn't tell you because we were truly afraid of you being depressed again. You know how difficult it was to see you that way and to not be able to do anything," he starts; I can feel the pain in his voice.

"Since when?" I say. As he looks confused, I add, "Since when did you decide this?"

"Last year. We both decided that it has to stop as we don't love each other any more. Besides, your mother loves someone else. She told me from the beginning. And Marc accepted that we keep acting like the perfect family for your mental health. The divorce has taken a year; we're finally done. We wanted to tell you, but you looked so happy with Shawn in your life and—"

"Is this why you're so okay with him?" I snap in a hurt voice.

"No. I really like him, if not I would never let him near you."

"I am so—"

"Please," I cut my mother off again. "So, what are we doing now?" I say in a whisper, clapping my hands together.

"Your mother will move in with Marc after Christmas, so you'll live here with me. But you can visit her when you want or even live with them," he answers, watching me to see how I take the news.

"Good. Thank you."

I stand up and walk back to my room, acting like I am indifferent to this. When I step into my room, I let out a long breath and sit on the edge of my bed. I grab my box of pictures and look at our family photos. So, my doubts have been confirmed; they don't love each other or they have stopped. I don't know why I am mad at my mother, maybe because she's the woman and they taught me that women are the ones who are supposed to fix these problems, to keep their relationship alive. Maybe that's not true and it's all lies; maybe she has the right to love who she wants. Still, I am mad at her because she could have tried more; she could have tried to save her marriage. But anyway, I am not a child any more and if they have decided to divorce, it is their choice and not mine. I can't force them to stay together; I am just asking them to be honest with me. I thought that once done with my depression, it would be in the past, but apparently it is not going to be as I expected. It's something that will stay in their minds and in mine and will always be part of our family.

***

"What did you get for Shawn?" Kate asks me. I am with Kate and Caroline in a Starbucks at the mall. Before our exams, we decided to go Christmas shopping. That way, we won't suffer the long lines at the last moment.

"I got some books about architecture for my dad and some tools he wants. I got the heels I showed you for my mother," I answer, distracted by the crowd.

"First, it's very nice of you to get something for your mother," Caroline starts. "And second, we want to know what you bought for Shawn."

I roll my eyes and take a sip of my drink. Kate and I have ordered chipotle chicken sandwich, Caroline ordered a roasted butternut squash kale salad. I have a caramel macchiato and the twins are drinking coffee. Caroline bought some 80s music videos for Tom and she is planning to knit a sweater for him — yes, she knows how to knit. Kate doesn't want to say what she bought for Chester either.

"I don't know why I should tell you, while you're also keeping secret what you bought for Chester," I argue, making her roll her eyes.

"Because." This is the only thing she can say anyway.

We finally talk about other things: exams, how we are going to spend Christmas.

"You're seriously going to that party?" Caroline asks, wide-eyed with surprise. I shrug.

"Yes, it'll be a great way to destress after exams and before going on that trip with my parents, Shawn and Frida. My mother invited Marc, can you imagine that?"

"Maybe you'll like him," Kate tries to calm me down.

"I liked him when I didn't know he was eating my mother's face," I reply, pouting like a four-year-old child but this is how I feel.

"But the party is before the exams, don't you know that?" Caroline states. "Ryan's family is travelling right after exams, so he has to have it before."

"Oh."

"But you can still come, it'll be Friday night anyway," Kate adds.

"I'll think about it," I tell them.

CHAPTER TWENTY-SEVEN

*"*A re you ready?"
I glance at Shawn and exhale. "Sure." He looks me up and down. I feel a kind of desire grow inside him, making me both uncomfortable and confident. I am so different from the Fifa who had no confidence in herself or her body. In three months, Shawn has helped me know my true self.

"What about your outfit? You're sure you don't want to change it?" I frown, confused. I'm wearing a red bodycon jumpsuit with black crepe heels. My hair is down on my shoulders, and I am wearing discreet makeup.

"I thought you liked it."

He scans my body once more and runs his hand through his hair. He sighs, "Yes, I do. Geez, I do. And I'm sure other boys at that party will also."

A smirk appears on my face as I say playfully, "You're so possessive." He rolls his eyes.

"Anyway, they'd better not to touch you." After that, he starts the car to drive to Ryan's for the Christmas party.

I remember when Ryan asked me if I could help them clean after this party. I know that he didn't specifically invite me for it but just wanted me to clean. How kind of him! The old Fifa would have thought like this: *maybe if I do that, his friends and him are going to like me and that will help me to forget about the past.* But today, I don't really care about being liked by anyone else because I already have people who truly care for me. When Shawn stops on the driveway, we glance at each other as if we were going to meet the Queen of England. This party is really stressing me out; I don't get why. I hope it all goes well tonight.

There are already people drunk outside, some are leering at me and I instantly regret dressing so sexily. My hand is in Shawn's as we walk into the big house. People call it "the party house" at college. They say that lots of things happen here and that you never leave one of these parties with whom you arrived. Some people are exchanging saliva in the most disturbing way.

"Ready for your first real party?" Shawn asks me, squeezing my hand.

I exhale once more before nodding. "I think so."

In high school, I was never invited to any parties. They all thought I was going to kill the mood; I was not even that depressed. We ring the bell like anyone else would. Surprisingly, Dylan is the one to open a few seconds later. A huge smile appears on his face while he leers at my body and then at Shawn before running his tongue over his bottom lip. Shawn's hold on my hand becomes tighter. I pray that he will control himself. Shawn's far from a violent guy but I'm not sure he'll play nice with Dylan if he tries anything.

"Fifa and loser. Welcome," he slurs drunkenly.

I smile at him and quickly pull Shawn inside. The music inside is very loud and most people are dancing or just talking. Some are already dead drunk, lying on the floor or throwing up. I don't really like those ogling stares at me and I will definitely not wear this kind of clothes any more again. We meet Ryan who hands us red cups.

"Fifa, glad to see you," he welcomes us warmly. I am surprised he even remembers my name. We thank him before walking over to the twins who are next to the snack stands.

"Hey," Kate says before pulling us in for a hug.

"You're hot," Caroline continues and hugs us. "Shawn... always great. You look strangely tense. Fif, you have to relax," Caroline makes fun of me. I roll my eyes.

"What do you have here?" Kate asks looking into our cups. "Beer? It's disgusting. Let's try some cocktails." She doesn't wait for our answer and takes the red cups from me. She gives me another one with a colored liquid in it. "Don't worry, the only alcohol in this is vodka," she specifies.

I take a bit of it; it's very tasty, a little sweet.

"It's good, huh?" Caroline asks for my opinion.

I nod and they both smile. Chester arrives behind us and wraps his arms around Shawn and my' shoulders. "Hey guys."

"Chester," I say. As usual, he looks like the one having the most fun at this party, his cheeks are pink and his eyes, bright.

"Ready for a party game?" Shawn asks me and I nod. I drink the whole of my drink in one go. "You should go slow with the alcohol though," he advises me, brows furrowed.

I roll my eyes before taking his drink that I also drink in one gulp.

"Oh! Fifa!" Chester chuckles, tipsy.

We walk into the room he leads us to and stop at a table where people are throwing balls into cups and drinking.

"We call this beer pong," Chester tells me.

"We should maybe avoid games that can get her drunk," Shawn warns Chester who scoffs, waving his hand dismissively.

"It's a party, she has to get drunk. We all know you don't drink much and never get drunk at parties, but a drunk Fifa is so cool. So, let her decide for herself."

The twins laugh while Shawn sighs. "Relax," I whisper against his ear before kissing him.

I am standing at one side of the table with Caroline; Chester and Kate are on the other side with Liam.

"Dude, are you playing or not?" Liam asks Shawn, doing some weird stretches.

"I think someone has to be sober," he declines.

"Fine. Caro and Fifa, you should find someone to add to your team," Chester shouts to get heard over the loud music.

I quickly look around and spot a guy. "Hey come here," I shout to him, giggling. At first taken aback, he finally shrugs before joining us.

"I told you that drunk Fifa is cool and she is not even that drunk yet." Chester throws the first ball which lands in the cup. "Are you ready to lose?" he speaks directly to me, raising his arms.

"Are you ready to?" I reply competitively. When I throw for the first time, the ball bounces to the side. I drink a cup of beer while Chester smirks. I avoid Shawn's gaze because I know that he is not okay with this. However, I just want to act without thinking about consequences for once. After lots of cups of beer, Chester's team finally wins. I feel a little dizzy and heat is growing inside me but I still want more and more alcohol.

"Loser," Chester teases me making the sign with his finger and thumb.

"I will take my revenge, don't worry. But for now, let's dance," I say loudly, over-excitedly. Everyone around me shouts, already moving their bodies to the music. We head to the dancefloor and I pull Shawn with me. This time he is free. We are all dancing and moving. Okay, we are actually throwing our arms around, but this is brilliantly awful dancing. Chester lifts me onto his shoulders and spins himself round while I shout, singing and giggling. Shawn removes me from his shoulders, and I wrap my legs around his waist and kiss him with tongue. I would have never imagined that I could kiss someone this way, in public. Everyone says "Oooh". I laugh, and so does Shawn eventually.

Shawn finally puts me down and we continue dancing. The song is "Gangnam Style" by PSY. We are all jumping around. Chester even throws himself on the floor, lying on the back and Kate climbs on him while dancing. We are all going crazy, I think.

To my great surprise, the D.J. puts on some Nigerian music and the *shaku shaku*, the only dance I have actually mastered fits perfectly to it. "Hey guys," I shout and everyone stops to look at me. "Let me teach you a dance," I say again and they all shout excitedly. I stand in the middle of the crowd and dance like I never have before to "Science Student" by Olamide and after that to "Freedom" by Shatta Wale, followed by my new students. At the end of the dance, I shout again, "Yeah" and they all reply.

"I'm going to the bathroom," I whisper to Shawn.

"Be careful," he says and I nod. I walk as normally as I can trying not to fall down.

"Move I want to pee," I shout to people on my way.

They look at me whether weirdly or amused, I'm not sure. When I get to the corridor, I walk faster and hold my lower stomach breathing noisily. "I'll pee in this corridor if I don't find the damn bathroom now." I finally find it and run to the toilet. I don't sit down, but hover over it, because I don't know whose buttocks or any other part of the body have been there. When I am done, I wash my hands and look at myself in the mirror. I wink and kiss the air and then I giggle. As I walk out of the bathroom, someone touches my ass. I turn to slap them but they grab my wrist. Dylan?

"What do you want?" I try to escape but he doesn't let go.

"Just to have some fun. You drive me crazy," he answers with a leer, pulling me closer. The smell of alcohol on his breath makes me sick.

"I don't want to, leave me alone." I push him but he persists. He holds me against the wall, slides his hand between my thighs. I push him and try to kick him, but he holds my arms above my head.

"Leave me alone. Help!" I shout. He laughs drunkenly before pressing his lips to mine. Tears are flowing down my cheeks as I shout and bite at him, but he doesn't want to let me go.

"You thought you would come here and turn us on and go away just like that?" he scowls, tightening his hold.

He kisses my neck and I feel the disgust grow and grow inside me.

"Fifa?"

"Are you crazy, kissing me like that?" Dylan hisses abruptly as he backs away. My brain is still processing the situation. My eyes meet Shawn's running towards us. In a blink, he is already standing over Dylan, punching him violently.

"Shawn no, no," I beg him.

"Dylan!" Oh great! It's Hailey. She runs to them and tries to push Shawn away; his knuckles are busted as his chest heaves. He is flushed with anger while Dylan's face is all messed up. His lip is split and blood is flowing from his broken nose. Shawn finally stands up, fists clenched. He looks once again at all of us. I read a tension in his eyes, as if he's disappointed or hurt. Can he possibly believe that I was kissing Dylan? He walks quickly away. I am paralyzed, not moving. I am still wondering what would have happened if Shawn hadn't shown up, what is going to happen now. "Oh baby," Hailey whines while hugging Dylan who is playing the victim. Then she turns on me. "You bitch, what did you do to my man?"

"What did I do? He just tried to rape me," I shout at her, furious.

"She jumped on me," Dylan protests with an innocent voice. I shake my head in disbelief.

"Don't worry, I believe you baby. We'll take our revenge. Your boyfriend will pay." How can she believe him?

"It's fine if you want to believe him while he doesn't even give a shit about you. But don't you dare touch Shawn," I scream, pointing my finger at them. "Just leave him alone. His grandmother is sick and she only has him. They don't need any trouble. Don't you have any sympathy?" I don't know why I am telling them that. Maybe expecting some feeling of guilt from them, but nothing. "You know what? Fuck you," I hiss and walk away.

When I enter the living room, everyone shouts my name energetically. Minutes earlier I had been doing my one woman show, laughing and partying. Now I'm on the verge of crying and throwing up everything in my stomach. My head is spinning but I have to find Shawn. "Where is Shawn?" I ask Liam desperately.

"I don't know," he furrows his brows at me, "Are you okay?"

"Yes, yes."

215

I look around but don't see him. I leave the house to finally find him leaning against the car. "Shawn I'm so sorry," I start, sobbing. His features harden as he goes to get in his car, taking no notice of me. I grab his shirt, and he turns to me violently.

"I told you to not get drunk. I told you to be careful," he shouts, waving his arms, his voice cracked. "What did you want to prove? That you can be like them? Just imagine that he had done something to you." His voice breaks with a sob at the last part.

"I'm sorry," I repeat quietly, staring at my feet.

"You'd better be," he finishes, giving me a look that is so full of disappointment that I can't even bear it.

He gets in the car, looking straight in front of him. I presume that he is waiting for me to get in, so I do, quietly. He drives in silence, a heavy and uncomfortable silence. I glance at him from time to time, but he doesn't give me a single look. He still looks angry, tense fingers around the steering wheel. No music in the car. When he finally stops on my driveway, I glance once again at him, expecting some look or a kiss or a smile or anything, but nothing.

"Shawn, please."

"Just go please. It's fine."

I sigh and get out of the car, leaving a piece of my heart inside. I walk straight to the bathroom and fall down by the toilet. I vomit up the whole content of my stomach. I think I even vomit the lining my stomach itself. I am crying and sobbing, not able to stop the pain that's growing inside me. I acted like a slut. I just wanted to party, to have fun, nothing more, but I put myself in danger. I am so stupid. My mother walks in.

"Oh my God," she winces, "Darling."

She kneels down next to me, removes my hair from my face, holding it back. I don't have the strength to fight her this time. I want her to be here. I want my mother. "Shawn hates me," I cry before vomiting again.

"He would never do that," she tries to reassure me.

I rest my head on the toilet seat, "I got drunk. Even though he warned me and told me to be careful. I didn't listen to him," I fall silent for a while, sniffing, "Dylan tried to force me to have sex with him. Shawn beat him up and..." I burst into tears. My mother doesn't look at all disgusted by me or by the contents of the toilet. I guess she has seen worse as a mother and as a doctor.

"He's not mad at you but at himself and at Dylan. Tomorrow, you'll see that everything will be fine," she promises me softly.

"Why do I always ruin everything?" I say in a whisper, staring blankly at nothing.

"You don't sweetie," I hear her say before I fall asleep.

***

Today is the first exam day. The day after the party, I woke up in my bed with an incredible hangover. My mother had changed my clothes the night before and when I woke up, I found breakfast next to my bed with some pills. I know she feels guilty, but I also know that she loves me. I tried to text Shawn throughout the weekend; he answered but he was cold and distant in his replies. He said that we would talk after the exams, before we go to my father's chalet. I'm relieved that he still wants to talk to me. So, I try to concentrate on the exams. I only see Shawn in class and obviously we can't talk.

***

Today is the last exam day. Everyone is happy and relieved, especially because of the short holiday. But I am even happier to know that I am finally going to talk with Shawn. As I walk out of the class, I spot some people gathered around a wall. There are pictures on the walls, all along the hallway. My heart starts beating fast, warning me that this isn't good. When I walk into the hallway, some of the people stare at me. Some are laughing while some look sympathetic. I finally glance at a picture and my heart sinks. I breathe loudly, my hand covers my mouth in horror. My brain literally stops working. This is a dream, a bad dream. There are photos of Frida. The things written on them are awful. *Sick ma'am, sick grandson. As blind as the grandson. Can she at least see how stupid her grandson is? When is she going to die?*

I back away, hopelessly trying to catch my breath. I told them about her, I gave them the means to hurt him. Tears are falling on my cheeks. I close my eyes. When I close them, I see myself much younger, in elementary school. Someone draws me with a very black crayon and everyone laughs at me. He pastes the picture on the wall. *Thin as a rake, black as coal.* I see myself trying to wash away my brown complexion, with soap, with a pumice stone. I see myself shouting and crying. I remember that day that broke me.

I scream in the hallway, savagely tearing down the pictures. I storm over to Dylan and Hailey who are smiling smugly; I throw the pictures at them. "Why? Why are you so cruel? How can you make fun of this?" I scream, my voice broken.

"We just wanted to share the information you gave us," Dylan says with a smirk, shrugging. I feel my heart burn when Shawn looks at me from behind them, eyes red. He walks away.

"Shawn!" I shout and run after him, but he is faster.

He gets into his car, slams the door shut and drives away. Tears are falling and falling, and my soul is breaking and breaking. When I drive home, I throw myself on the couch, sobbing. I call Shawn but he doesn't pick up. I went to his place before coming home; I rang the bell in a frenzy. Frida's nurse opened and said that he was not back.

I try to call him the whole day; I text him but he never answers. I think this time, I have lost him for good.

CHAPTER TWENTY-EIGHT

The next day is the day of the family trip. I pack my bags, wondering if Shawn will show up. Shawn and Frida are not going any more, I'm pretty sure of it. When I get downstairs, I see them in the living room and blink several times, to be sure that I'm not dreaming. Shawn looks away. Surely noticing it, my parents look sadly at me.

"Let's go," Father says.

"Marc will join us there," my mother tells me and I just nod. I don't have enough space in my brain to process so many problems at the same time. I am going to spend Christmas with my mother and her boyfriend, my father, my angry boyfriend (if he still is) and his grandmother.

During the journey, which take hours, I watch the scenery. I don't try to look at Shawn because I know he will avoid eye contact with me. The hours seem so long and painful. Tomorrow is Christmas. The worse Christmas of my life. When we arrive, it's already evening so everyone is tired. The caretaker of the chalet comes to meet us and we greet him. He helps us with the luggage.

"I'm so excited" Frida exclaims.

I know why Shawn came. He wants her to enjoy, as much as possible, the rest of her life. She can't easily use her cane with all this snow, so I help her to the door. When we are all inside, it's warm and comfortable. It has been years we were last here and the place hasn't changed. After settling in, I cook something quick with my mother and we have dinner. Frida is the lively one, talking about her trips and journeys, the countries she has visited and the countries she still wants to visit. I am looking at my plate, not feeling hungry. My stomach is knotted. I glance at Shawn; he seems to feel the same way. It's so hard to be so close to him but so far away. After dinner, he walks out of the chalet. I grabbed the nearest jacket, even though it's not a warm one and I know I'll freeze.

"Shawn," I say. He doesn't answer and just continues on his way. "Please." I walk faster and stop in front of him, I am dying of cold, but I don't care. "Talk to me."

"You want me to congratulate you for what you did?" he says in a sarcastic tone. Then he claps his hands together, his nose red.

"No. I swear that I told them to—"

"To make them have pity on me?" he cuts me off, "Didn't you tell me that you hate it when people pity you?"

"I..." A cold tear wets my face as my mouth stays open, because I don't know what to say. But I have to say something, anything. He walks back inside the chalet, leaving me, standing in the freezing cold. Finally, I go inside.

"What were you doing outside at this time and in this freezing cold?" my mother asks me, and I give her a sad look that tells her why. She gently strokes my hair as we sit at the counter in the kitchen. She makes me a hot chocolate.

"Where is Marc?" I ask her eventually.

"He's coming tomorrow. He got an urgent case."

I bury my gaze into the liquid in the cup. "You love him?"

"Yes, I do."

I sigh and take a sip of my drink before saying, "Then I wish you happiness."

She hugs me; I hug her back and she kisses my cheek. "We'll always be a family," she whispers, crying.

Christmas Day, we are all in the living room around the big Christmas tree. Walter, the caretaker, has done a great job. Our breakfast is on the low table. Walter opens the door to Marc. My mother stands up, walks over to him and she kisses him after a long hug. "Sorry I'm late," he apologizes. "Merry Christmas everyone."

"Merry Christmas." My father walks to him and they shake hands. I also stand up slowly. Three of them have their apprehensive gazes on me as I slowly walk to Marc. He pulls me in for a hug.

"Fifa candy," he calls me the same way he used to when I was younger. I smile at him.

We have breakfast. Frida, Marc and my parents are laughing and talking. I just stare at the cup in my hand, silently. We finally exchange gifts. I don't give mine to Shawn yet. I want it to be special, even if it's not certain that I'll get a time to give it to him.

"You know me so well," my father says when I give him my gift and I giggle. You can give him anything as long as it's about architecture and he will be happy.

I give an MP4 player to Frida. I have specially selected some music and comedy shows for her. "For you to laugh at any time," I whisper to her.

"Thank you, darling."

Shawn doesn't give me anything. I guess he hasn't bought anything for me at all. After breakfast, we all just hang out together. Frida wants to make a snowman.

"Let me help you," I tell her. We protect ourselves against the cold and grab some equipment.

"Aren't you coming Shawn?" she asks him. "Come, please."

I bite my bottom lip and just help Frida to walk through the snow. I start to make the first ball.

"Let me roll it," she says, kneeling in the snow like a child. I gently pull it to her and put her hands on it. Shawn is silently doing his own while I am staring at him. He catches me and I look away.

"You guys are so quiet. What's going on?"

"Nothing, Grandma," Shawn says quickly. When we are finally done, she runs her hands over the snowman.

"This is beautiful" she says, and I smile, rubbing my hand on her back. This woman is a sunshine.

We have lunch and later we have dinner, as Christmas flies by.

"Mrs Tremblay told me they expelled Dylan and Hailey from school. What did they do?" Father asks me during dinner and I almost choke on my food. Shawn is suddenly interested in me. His eyes are on me and I want to bury myself in the snow.

I clear my throat. "They misbehaved," I answer quietly, staring at my food.

"They always do anyway," Father shrugs.

"Yes."

"Maybe people shouldn't encourage them to keep doing it," Shawn suddenly speaks up accusingly, once again I almost choke.

"Maybe those people are innocent, and they just care about those they love," I reply, biting the inside of my cheeks. Everyone is uncomfortable, shifting in their seats but I don't really mind their presence for now.

"Love has nothing to do with pity," he hisses and I stand up clumsily.

"Excuse me," I say before walking out.

I walk and walk in the snow, holding back my tears. I find a place and sit there alone. Once again, I am just wearing a jacket. I stay there for a while, processing that I have lost Shawn. Someone puts a blanket around me, and I lift my head up to see Shawn.

"I'm sorry," he says, and I frown. Why is he sorry?

He sits next to me and we stay silent, contemplating the winter sky, wistful and beautiful. Then, I decide that this is the moment to tell him everything.

"When we moved here, I was always sick," I start quietly, "People didn't like me at school. I was always smiling at them and laughing and joking but they just seemed to not like me. I wasn't growing the same as the other children: my muscles were weak; I was too thin and I'm black." I fall silent for a while, remembering how difficult it was for an eight years old girl to live with that. When he locks our fingers together, I look up at him and then back at the sky. "One day, someone drew a horrible picture of me and they all made fun of me. They called me names. Thin as a rake. Black as coal. There were other black people in my school, but they chose only me to make fun of. And the saddest part is that even the other black children were part of it. Kids can be so cruel. That day, something broke inside me. When I went back home, from that day, I stopped smiling and eating, and I was depressed for years." I'm crying but trying to keep speaking. I have to tell him everything. "I was trying my best in school so my parents and everyone else wouldn't feel alarmed. At some point I started acting like I was fine again. I was afraid to let everything out. I was bullied and disliked. When my growing miraculously started again and my curves started appearing, I thought I would be okay but I couldn't be happy any more." My heart is burning in my chest; I'm reliving each bit of those days. Those dark days. "When I saw what they did to Frida, I saw myself years ago and I felt bad," I finally finish in a whisper.

He turns to me, hugs me tightly, my face against his chest. I sob and cry freely against him. I let everything out. I feel so well, like weight is lifting from my shoulders.

"Let's go back inside before we freeze out here," he finally says as we both smile to each other.

He stands, gives me his hand and we walk to the chalet. He leads me to his room. The warmth of the place calms me and makes me feel better. I leave my jacket on the floor, and we remove our shoes and throw ourselves on the bed. He wraps his arm around my shoulder to make me lean against his side. I bury my head in the hollow of his neck, feeling good. Then I remember that I haven't given him his present. I go to my room and come back with it. I hand him the small notebook.

"What is it?" he asks as he opens it.

"A memory book. I put our pictures in, with the group or our family on some pages. I wrote something for you with each one," I tell him, smiling.

He stops on the page where there is a picture of us, eating the same spaghetti, that day we kissed for the whole restaurant to see. A smile finds its way to his lips.

"Thank you, baby," he starts, making my inside melt, "I don't know if my gift will be as good," he adds.

My eyes go wide, "You bought me something?"

"Of course. I bought two VIP tickets for the Shawn Mendes concert." He hasn't finished his sentence before I jump into his lap, kissing him all over his face.

"Thank you, thank you," I sing; we laugh, the melodious song of our mingled laughter filling the room.

Then we start kissing. I had missed his lips; I feel like we haven't kissed for years; this feels so good. He bites my bottom lip, plays with my tongue, moves his hands on my body, cuddles me, kisses me. We finally fall asleep in each other's arms, peaceful.

The next day, when we get downstairs, talking and laughing, everyone's eyes are on us. They look taken aback at first, but they smile at us. Frida is sitting on the couch, already listening to the music on her new possession. This is my new family, my lovely family. In this actual moment, right here, I know that I'm healing.

CHAPTER TWENTY-NINE

M arc puts the last bags in the trunk before closing it. Mother walks over to me, a sad look on her face but she smiles at me, hands in the pockets of her large coat. No snow today, but the weather is still freezing. I sneeze both because of my crying and the cold. I can't believe that she is leaving. My mother is leaving. She is going to build a new family and maybe have new kids since she is below fifty and as she is probably still young enough, I guess.

It's now going to be just my father and me. I have a special relationship with my mother, the kind of relationship I can't have with Dad. The same way I can't have the kind of relationship I have with Daddy with Mother. I need both, equally. She stops in front of me and I wrap my arms around her shoulders to hug her. I hug her tightly, like I never want her to go. I want my parents with me, forever. But we are supposed to separate one day anyway. The love we have for one another will last forever. One day, I will get to live with a new person and build my own family. She kisses my face, telling me that she loves me. I say that I love her too.

"We're not living that far away. You can come by whenever you want. It'll also be your house. I'll come and pick you up very soon," she assures me softly.

I smile at her, glancing at Marc who is watching us, leaning against his car, his arms crossed over his chest. I know he loves her. By the way they look at each other, the same way I once saw Daddy and her look at each other. However, in all honesty, Marc and Mother are really in love, in a way my parents have never been. I know it by the way he takes care of her, the way he protects her like she's the most precious thing ever. He is good for her, perfectly good for her. I just hope it will last and that she will be happy. "Don't you dare prefer your future children," I warn her, pointing my finger at her as she laughs.

"I won't dare. You're my most precious gift," she reassures me before hugging me again. I love being her little girl, at thirty, forty, fifty and over, I will still be her girl, her baby girl. The one whose hair she took care of and braided (I cried buckets), the one she took to bed when she fell asleep on the couch in front of the TV, the one she loves.

Daddy comes out of the house with a smile on his face. He also looks a little sad. He hugs my mother. "So… goodbye," she finally says, stepping back.

Daddy wraps his arm around my shoulder and I lean against him, trying to not cry any more. We wave at Marc who waves back at us with a smile and then, they leave, mother blowing me kisses till they disappear. I hug Dad, sobbing as he pats my head and comforts me. We walk back inside. The house already looks empty. But I guess, life is this: change. Changes make life and life is a perpetual change. Nothing is really meant to last; we just have to enjoy each moment. I don't know if I really enjoyed Mother but she's just few blocks away. I promise that I will take care of what I still have, cherish those I love, till my lungs give out. Depression didn't tell me that before. She never told me that my life was wonderful. She never told me that I deserve the best and that I have to fight for it and enjoy it. Happiness is telling me all that. I know that I will sometimes have to cry and be sad but this is also part of life. Then, I will smile, smile till my cheeks hurt.

I sit in front of the TV to watch Sponge Bob. I receive a text from Shawn at a really funny part of the show.

Please, come.

I don't know why, but I start to stress as soon as I read this. This doesn't feel good at all. I slip my feet into my flats and quickly get in my car. On Shawn's driveway, I quickly get out. He is standing on the porch, arms dangling beside his body, the door open behind him. He looks empty. I frown and run to him. "What's wrong?" I ask him, swallowing with difficulty.

"She left me." His voice cracks but he doesn't cry. I take a step back; my mouth falls open. I understand. My heart sinks. Shawn looks lost, lost forever. I walk towards him, but he just walks away to let me in the house. Frida is lying on the couch, eyes open. Her mouth is slightly open but smiling. The headphones are in her ears and the MP4 player is on her chest. When I step closer, I notice that she was listening to "Forever Young", One Direction's version. I turn to Shawn who is behind me and I hug him. I hug him as hard as I can. The sirens of the ambulance rings through the neighborhood and paramedics enter minutes later. I show them Frida's body because Shawn can't talk. They take care of her.

They put her body into a bag as if she were not a person. Is life this fragile? One second, she was lying and listening to music and just after she's dead. I can't imagine how Shawn felt when he saw this, when he tried to wake her up, but she didn't move.

***

Today's the thirty-first December. But today's also Frida's burial. We are saying goodbye to her, to the year and to these last moments. All dressed in black, we are standing in the cemetery, around her grave. There is Shawn's group of friends, my family, Alicio's family, Hassan, Theresa and some people I don't know. The moment seems real. We are really saying goodbye to her, forever. Frida wanted to be forever young; she enjoyed every moment. That's why that trip was so important to her; it was a last pleasure in her life. She wanted to enjoy it till the last second.

"Today, we're saying goodbye to Frida Davis, a mother, a grandmother, a sister, a friend. We'll all remember how special she was. How dear to our heart she was," starts the priest in a ceremonial tone. After him, Shawn, Alessia and I give little speeches, hoping that Frida would hear us from heaven. It's freezing cold, but nobody seems to really mind it. Shawn is silent, so silent since what happened. He has not even cried.

After the ceremony, people hug him and offer their condolences. It's now just the two of us, in front of the grave, next to the rest of his family.

"So here is my family, in a cemetery," Shawn says blankly.

I don't know what to reply. "You know they loved you and you know that you'll always love them. Again, you know there are still people loving you," I tell him, squeezing his hand. We face each other. "You know that you have the right to cry, don't you?" I add and he looks away. He needs it; he needs to let everything out. I put my hand softly on his cheek. "Happiness needs sadness. You have to get over sadness, if not your happiness will just be pretend. I won't judge you, Shawn."

He looks once again at me before kneeling down. He places his head in his hands. "I've tried. I tried to be happy, to be strong for them," he says and his voice cracks again. Tears are falling on his cheeks as sobs tear at his throat. Then I understand something. Shawn needs me as much as I need him. I was a sad person hiding her feelings. He is a hurt person hiding his feelings with smiles. Seeing him so vulnerable on the floor makes me acknowledge it. Shawn is hurt, deeply hurt. Because all his family has left him. He feels abandoned.

"And they're surely proud of you, Shawn. You're the greatest person I've ever met. You can be sad. It's your right, you're human. It's not a weakness. It doesn't mean that you'll be depressed," I wrap my arms around him and rest my forehead on his, "There are better things to come." He shakes and cries harder.

"I'll miss her. I still miss all of them. I can't," he cries, "You said that she'd be okay." My heart breaks. I lift his head up to me, making him look at me. His eyes are red.

"You can. I'll be there for you. You don't have to stop loving them or to forget them. Just keep on and enjoy your life, the same way Frida did." My cheeks are now as wet as my shaky hands stroking his cheeks are. "I'll love you as much and as long as I can, till my lungs give out. I promise you that I won't let you down, Shawn."

His face lights up a little as he looks up at me. I just said that I love him and it's true, I can't deny it. "I love you too," he replies with a small smile.

I bury my head in the hollow of his neck, sniffing. Shawn lets out all the tears he has been holding in for years. He is reborn, letting himself go. I hug him harder, falling on my knees. I kiss him with love and passion. I promise him love and hope and more love. We stay there for a long time, sitting on the floor. We finally get up, hand in hand. I smile to him and he smiles to me. And I love him. Because he is Shawn and because I can't even give reasons. But I know for sure that he made me smile. But then, I made him cry. Love must complete us, complete what is missing.

"Tip twelve for happiness: love," I whisper, and he smiles.

"Tip twelve for Shawn's happiness: love Fifa," he adds.

I chuckle as we walk out, hand in hand. No matter what happens next, I know that Shawn Davis, alias my savior, has changed my life in all possible and impossible ways. Tomorrow is a new day, but also a new year. A new beginning. And I just want us to be together, through happiness and sadness. Together, forever.

EPILOGUE

The Funny Food is full tonight; everyone wants to start the new year in a good atmosphere. Shawn's eyes are still red from crying, but he had to come, for this beautiful memorial in honor of Mia and Frida, the sunshine of this place.

Shawn and I are sitting at a table in a corner, as I glance at the people there. Hassan and Theresa are sitting with the group, my parents are sitting with Alicio and his wife. Two pictures are hanging on the wall beyond the big stage: Mia and Frida, with their most beautiful smiles. Shawn has asked me this morning, as soon as we left the cemetery, to live with him; I couldn't say no, I could only say yes. I feel that feeling, that feeling that makes you want to be with someone each moment of your fragile life, to never be far from the one, to breathe the one's name. Love. I squeeze Shawn's hand and smile to him. He gives me a sad smile, and I kiss his hand.

"Three, two, one…" everyone shouts around us, but the time seems to freeze for us.

"Happy New Year, Shawn," I say, softly, squeezing his hand.

He glances at the two photos; a tear falls from his eye again as he turns to me. "Happy New Year, baby."

I give him a gentle kiss. I know that he won't heal overnight, but I know how strong Shawn is. Some pains are just unbearable, but I am here, right next to him to bear it with him.

"I love you," I whisper to him.

Our fingers are intertwined, he rubs his thumb over the back of my hand and looks at me, "I love you, forever. But I wish and beg the stars to die before you."